DRONE

An Eli Quinn Mystery

Robert Roy Britt

Published by Ink • Spot
P.O. Box 74693
Phoenix, Arizona 85087
InkSpotBooks.com
Published in the United States of America
First printing, 2016

Cover by Trent Design

This is a work of fiction. Names, places, characters and events are
imaginary or used fictitiously. Any resemblance to real people, places,
companies or events is totally coincidental.

Drone/Robert Roy Britt. 1st ed.
ISBN 978-0-9977614-0-5

Praise for the Eli Quinn Mystery Series

DRONE

"A brisk detective novel sequel that packs a punch."
— *Kirkus Reviews*

"Fast-paced with a few thought-provoking twists, DRONE is reminiscent of a noir detective story with a 21st century flair." (5 Stars)
— *IndieReader*

"Author Robert Roy Britt's writing is engaging and captivating—written both with a mature slant and just a little camp. Britt takes on a well-trod genre and introduces a distinct yet fitting addition to its hall of fame. Both brilliant and humble, hard-nosed and gentle, Eli Quinn's mettle is thoroughly tested in curious and entertaining ways. It's hard to make an original detective, but Britt is more than up to the challenge. He does a wonderful job of telling this twisting tale with excellent pace."
— *Self-Publishing Review*

CLOSURE

"Quinn's narrative often sports the hardened cynicism of a seasoned veteran ... Solo nearly steals the story; he can intimidate with a single bark and a follow-up growl."
— *Kirkus Reviews*

"Fascinating plot."
"Great characters."
"A great read."
— *Amazon Readers*

For Nadine. Always.

CHAPTER 1

I sat waiting for a client in my new office, just north of the corner of Pleasant Way and Easy Street. Trouble was, I didn't have any clients. I'd had just one case so far. It wasn't pleasant, and it wasn't easy. There were a couple broken noses and a nasty, unnatural bend to an elbow. But none of the damage was to me, and I'd solved the case.

Solo was curled up in the corner, snoring. Pandora streamed Van Morrison's *Russian Roulette* from my iPhone to a Bluetooth speaker.

I sat in my new Aeron chair with my running shoes up on a refurbished oak desk. I just needed a John Wayne hat. Well, and some boots. Along the left wall was a brown leather couch with a coffee table made of Indonesian hardwood. None of the furniture in my new office matched, but it had rustic charm.

Bells rang as the front door flew open. Solo didn't bark, so I knew who it was. Plus, I was expecting her.

Samantha Marcos blew in, bright and fresh, like a promise. Solo sprang to his feet and tried to sprint, slipped on the brand new wood floors but finally got to her. Sam rewarded the 110-pound German shepherd with some serious scratching behind the ears, letting him lick her face.

"What's with the bells?" Sam tucked some of her straight black hair behind one ear.

"Don't want to be surprised," I said. "Bad guys, you know."

Sam laughed lightly. It was, as always, a delightful laugh that rearranged my insides.

"You watched too many Westerns," she said. "Place is looking good. I saw the sign out front."

Eli Quinn, Private Investigator.

"Fancy. And I see you got your license." She pointed at the framed Private Investigation Agency license on the wall behind me.

I nodded.

"And the dollar?" She pointed to the smaller framed item next to the license.

"The one Delores Bernstein gave me."

"Your first fee."

"My only fee."

"There will be more," Sam said.

"You think?"

"I know. We just need to do some marketing for you. The cases will come."

"Lots of bad things happening here in Pleasant," I said.

"Probably more than we know."

I shrugged. Then I thought of Jess. I did that sometimes when I was happiest. Jess had been gone for more than a year now. She didn't haunt me as much lately, but she checked in now and then, as if unsure what she thought about Sam and me. Or maybe she just needed to share the moment. Or maybe I needed to share it with her.

I turned the music off. The air conditioner, perched in the front window, worked hard, its rattle and hum filling the silence. Sam and I were OK with silence.

Sam put her hands in the back pockets of her jeans. She

wore simple leather sandals and a white V-neck tee, casual yet somehow elegant on her five-foot-six frame. Sam had athletic strength, olive skin that lay smooth over her muscles, which looked capable without bulging.

I crossed my arms and stared at her, sighed loudly, then looked away and stood up. Solo, sensing the tension, went back to his corner and curled up, kept one eye on us.

"Let's go, Quinn." Sam nodded at the door. "The senator is about to speak. I have to report on it. You need to get out there and shake some hands."

"Whoopie," I said.

***

The mid-morning heat in Pleasant, Arizona already bordered on unbearable. The forecast called for 108 degrees this afternoon. It felt like most of those degrees had already arrived.

I walked south with Sam on the shady east side of Pleasant Way on Old West wooden sidewalks, reconstructed to be much like what had been there a century before. We crossed Easy Street and passed in front of Funky Furniture. An eclectic mix of wood and iron tables and chairs spilled out into the parking lot.

State Senator Jackie Brand, a widely loved and loathed Independent, was in Pleasant to launch an initiative to end Maricopa County Sheriff Horace Otto's program targeting illegal immigrants. Otto locked them up on a former cattle ranch down in Mesa, where they endured days and days under hot tin roofs, no air conditioning, awaiting trial and likely deportation. It was all well documented. Sheriff Otto made a point of inviting reporters in to get a lot of pictures and video, boasting of his roundup as if the immigrants were in fact cattle.

Senator Brand announced the event weeks in advance. She chose Pleasant because the town was friendly to her message. Pleasant's population, more diverse than the state in general, had voted overwhelmingly for Brand in the last statewide election.

We passed Lulu's Grind. I wanted to duck in for a coffee. Lulu made the best coffee in Pleasant, maybe the best coffee in the whole country. I stayed with Sam.

At Happy Lane we stepped into the town's central traffic circle with its original cobblestones. The circle was closed off. A small podium was set up in the middle, in front of Ringo, the ancient, muscle-bound saguaro cactus involved in a legendary shootout in 1881.

Barricades kept the small crowd out in the traffic circle, a good twenty feet from the podium. Out of habit, I did a quick count, the way I'd learned to do as a reporter. Tally a batch of twenty, extrapolate it across the crowd. About one-forty or one-fifty, I figured. The TV vans were parked around the circle, satellite antennas poking into the sky. A TV helicopter hovered well up and to the south.

I left Sam as she weaved through the crowd to get to the front, near the barriers. She had a reporter's notebook in hand, would take notes the old fashioned way. The video crew from *The Arizona Republic* caught up to her. Colleagues of Sam. Former colleagues of mine. They would record the speech and upload it in full to AZCentral.com, so Sam had no reason to record the audio.

Sometimes I wondered if reporters were even needed nowadays. Everything was streamed, tweeted, periscoped, shared, liked, hated and fully critiqued before a journalist could sit down to write. It was one part of reporting I didn't miss—chasing the tail of social media, trying to remain relevant.

I stayed back, tagging along only because Sam Marcos asked me to. Meet and greet, start cultivating future clients. I like people well enough, but I'm not the Rotary-club type.

"If you're going to be a dick," Sam had said, "you have to stop being a dick." Sam was not afraid of words.

Jackie Brand approached the dark green podium—a well-worn, portable plywood contraption with a lectern mounted on it—and climbed the two steps. Crisp blue suit several shades lighter than the sky. The crowd clapped politely. Ringo the cactus towered behind her.

Several posse members ringed the crowd in the back. One sheriff's deputy was always in Pleasant, paid by the town on a contract basis. The dozen volunteers of the posse—all men, mostly in their sixties and retired from other law enforcement jobs—backed up the deputy and handled routine duties like crowd control and school crossings. Posse members were limited in how much they were to engage with a violent or potentially dangerous incident. They were highly skilled B-team for the sheriff's department, a support group, all working for free.

I spotted the regular deputy of the morning, one I knew well. Saw another deputy—no, sergeant, the stripes indicated—I'd never seen before, a large blond-haired weightlifter type. Crew cut. Ray-Bans. Arms crossed in a standoffish FBI posture. He'd be in charge, given his rank.

I found my friend Jack Beachum and moved over behind him. Beachum was in his early seventies. Still fit. Short, straight tan-colored hair that matched his posse uniform.

"Stick 'em up, Beach," I said.

Jack Beachum didn't move. "You're gonna get yourself shot, you don't be careful."

"I'd have knocked the gun out of your hand before you turned around."

"I'm still plenty quick," Beach said. He turned slowly and made a gun shape with his thumb and finger, pulled the trigger.

"I see you're out in force today," I said. "I thought you guys don't like Jackie Brand."

"Some of us don't," Beach said. "Me, I think she's a maverick, and I like mavericks. Plus she's right about this roundup thing. Ain't moral."

"You being defiant against your own boss?"

"I'm being human," Beach said. "Besides, I'm volunteer. I take orders, but I don't have to take shit. And I don't have to agree with the boss."

"Ha," I said. "You just keep being you, Beach. That's what you're good at."

"Thanks, Sundance."

Jackie Brand began speaking. The crowd quieted and tuned in. I tuned out. I agreed with most of what the state senator stood for, but I was the choir to her preaching today. Plus there were other things to notice, and I was a noticer of things.

The setup was odd. Brand was isolated, with just one of her aides, who was off the podium and a few feet behind her. The barricades kept the crowd well back. The two deputies and several posse members were behind the crowd. None of it meant anything. Just things I noticed.

"Looks like nobody's expecting any trouble," I said in a low voice.

"Friendly town we got here," Beach said. "Lasko there," he nodded toward the big blond-haired aviator-sunglass-wearing, muscle-bound sheriff's sergeant, "said stay to the back, be unobtrusive, let civil liberty have its day. Some BS like that. Anyway, he and his boys swept the town earlier. Entrance is blocked until the speech is done. Nobody's expecting trouble."

I saw a blur of movement out of the corner of my eye, something moving swiftly over the two-story storefronts, coming in from the southwest, a sound between a whoosh and a hum that you'd barely notice if you didn't see the thing. In the time it took me to register it as a drone the size of a large pizza box, the blur bore down on Jackie Brand. Before anyone could point and shout, the drone slammed into the podium and exploded. Pieces of plywood flew in all directions. The senator flew back and fell to the ground.

CHAPTER 2

My ears rang from the blast. State Senator Jackie Brand lay motionless on her back near the remains of the plywood podium, her smart blue suit splattered with blood. The posse converged. I couldn't tell how badly she was hurt.

People scattered every which way, ducking and running but unsure where to go. Some screamed, others covered their heads with their arms, looking up. The chaos took on a pattern and the spectators ended up on the sidewalks surrounding the town center. Posse members huddled around Jackie Brand and her aide, who was several feet away, sitting up but also bloodied. Two TV crews along with the cameraman from *The Arizona Republic* tried to decide whether to film the crowd or the senator, shouting at each other and pointing. Like fish in a school, they shuffled together toward Brand. Two posse members stepped in to keep them at a distance. Another knelt next to her.

Sam Marcos hadn't run. She stood near the barricade still, watching the action and taking notes. She turned, spotted me and ran over.

"Drone," I said.

"Yep." She looked skyward. "Posse needs to get these people out of here." She waved one hand toward the crowd.

I looked around, could not see Beach. But I knew where he'd be. I sprinted to the center of the traffic circle, hurdled the traffic barriers.

"Beach," I shouted. "It was a drone. Could be more. Need to clear the area."

Jack Beachum emerged from the center of the group of posse members crowded around the senator. Instructed another to call an ambulance. The crowd had gone quiet. Beach spoke with a commanding voice. "Everyone clear out, now!" He made a shooing motion in several directions.

The crowd rushed toward all four compass points along the streets that radiated from the circle. Within seconds the center of Pleasant was mostly deserted. Sam stood next to me. One of the posse members knelt by Jackie Brand, another next to her assistant. Lasko stood by his black and gold sheriff's car. Stone-faced, sunglasses hiding his eyes. Oddly relaxed. Almost disinterested.

The TV crews ignored the call to disperse. They'd filmed the crowd rushing out and now turned to point their cameras again at Jackie Brand.

This must be how it feels after a shootout. I glanced at Ringo, the saguaro that'd been party to the town's famous 1881 duel with Johnny Ringo and, some said, Doc Holliday. A scar covered a bullet said to be still embedded. Ringo had suffered no further damage today.

Everything was still and silent. There was no dust settling, but the heat felt hotter than before. The sky seemed sharper and a darker shade of blue. Jackie Brand hadn't moved. A siren wailed faintly in the distance. It would take a minute or two for the ambulance to enter Pleasant and make its way to the town center.

I wasn't sure why, but I knew it was over now. Lasko had seemed to know that, too. One drone. One target. Very little collateral damage other than a podium and the senator's assistant.

"No accident," I said to Sam.

"Assassination attempt," she said.

"Not just some nutjob."

"Maybe a nutjob. But one who plans meticulously."

"And knows how to pilot drones," I said.

"And build bombs."

"Very light bombs."

I had bought an off-the-shelf drone a couple years ago, a quadcopter with four plastic helicopter-like blades. Stable and easy to fly. Popular because a novice could fly the thing right out of the box. On command, it actually took off and hovered in place on its own. An onboard Wi-Fi connected it to an app on a smartphone, which served as the controller. It had a video camera that recorded everything in front of it. Simple and fun, but with the potential to be much more than an indoor toy that smacked into Christmas trees no matter where you tried to steer it.

I wasn't the only person who had done a lot of thinking about what else could be done with a drone. Like my friend, Pauly, who was deep into drones. He helped me build another one, more powerful yet quieter and more sophisticated. Flew it a few times. It was fast and maneuverable, with a longer range, but after learning the basics of flying and a few tricks, I got bored with it.

"Let's soup it up," Pauly had said.

But even his enthusiasm didn't keep me in it. As with a lot of other hobbies, I learned yet again that I didn't have the patience of a real do-it-yourselfer. Other hobbyists were building serious drones, downright scary machines that could fly higher, farther, carry a payload, and be controlled with pinpoint accuracy. The FAA was issuing regulations, but anyone who would put a bomb on a drone probably wasn't worried about those rules.

"Didn't get a very good look at it," I said to Sam. "But it wasn't an off-the-shelf model. Quadcopter. Bigger than most of the ones you see advertised. You have to practice a lot to fly one that accurately." I looked around at the skyline, a mix of two-story, Old West facades and modern, one-story stucco store fronts, all laid out in a perfect grid around the central traffic circle. Wondered if the pilot had been standing on a nearby roof, or maybe even was in the crowd. I logged in my mind the direction the drone had come from.

Lasko hadn't moved, still standing next to his car. He watched the scene, talking on his cell phone in a normal tone of voice. Law enforcement officers were trained to deal with crises. Jack Beachum had reacted well. The other posse members had reacted well. But none looked as calm as Sergeant Lasko. I made a mental note of that, too.

CHAPTER 3

All of the promised 108 degrees had settled in by mid-afternoon. My red Jeep Wrangler's top was down. As long as the Jeep was moving, the heat was bearable. I rarely put the top up, when it was raining or for a few weeks during the Arizona winter when temperatures in the Valley dipped into the forties overnight, sometimes lower.

I didn't have anything to do. I was no longer employed by *The Arizona Republic*, so I wasn't reporting on the day's biggest story, the apparent attempted assassination by drone of Arizona State Senator Jackie Brand, in critical condition at a nearby hospital. Meanwhile, I still didn't have any cases. Solo and I had gone home to eat lunch. Then I drove us back to the office.

I came in from the north on Pleasant Way, turned left across the northbound lane and angled into a parking spot in front of the office, just up from Funky Furniture and Lulu's Grind and within sight of the police tape that blocked off the traffic circle. Started to sweat as soon as I parked. Solo hopped out of the back and immediately heeled. We walked up onto the wooden sidewalk and into my office.

The bells on the door rang. Sam sat behind my big oak desk. Solo went straight to Sam, sat next to the Aeron chair—my one indulgence of expensive, modern furniture—and waited for a scratch behind the ears, which he got.

"Just filed," she said, closing her laptop and leaning back. "Thanks for letting me use your office."

"Glad it's getting some use."

The office was sixteen feet wide and slightly deeper. Along the back wall was a counter with a sink and coffee maker. A small fridge was tucked underneath. I sat in one of the two client chairs facing the desk. They were from World Market, made of low-grade leather and inexpensive light-colored wood stained dark to look richer. They were not particularly attractive, but I had picked them up at forty percent off, and they were comfortable.

I tried not to look directly at Sam. It was always hard to look at her without staring. A moment passed silently. I glanced up to find her studying me. Solo looked at me, too. Solo stayed by Sam.

Sam was the only person Solo would choose over me, ear scratch or not.

I was pretty sure Sam knew what I was thinking about. She always seemed to. I wondered if Solo did, too. Probably. I pressed my lips together. Not a smile, but an acknowledgement. I was confident Sam wouldn't rush me, wherever we were going with this. I leaned my head back and stared up at the open beams and the bare, ancient wood ceiling, eight-inch-wide planks that formed the floor of a hair studio above.

"I barely get going with this new private detective agency thing, and there's a bombing a block away, shuts down the town," I said.

Footsteps clicked above and the ceiling creaked.

"Not very good for business," Sam said.

"The pumps on my ceiling?"

"The bombing."

"Yeah, well, maybe Sheriff Otto will hire me." I got up, walked over to the fridge.

"I wouldn't count on that."

"Agreed. Otto would be glad to see Jackie Brand out of politics," I said.

"Been a thorn in his side for years."

"Makes you wonder," I said.

"Does."

"How is she?"

"In a coma," Sam said. "Down at the Mayo Clinic in Scottsdale. They're being tight-lipped, so I don't know much more than that."

"How about the assistant?"

"A nasty cut on the head, a few other scrapes, nothing major. Just a lot of bleeding. She'll be OK."

"Head wounds do that." I didn't have much to add. I pulled my iPhone out of its holster and launched Pandora. The same station that was playing hours ago started back up on the Bluetooth. Van Morrison sang:

And it seems like, yes it feels like

A brand new day, yeah

I opened the fridge, bent over and looked in. There was a six-pack of Sierra Nevada, a case of bottled water and some ketchup. The beer was calling. I took a water. "Want one?"

"Thanks," she said.

I tossed a bottle across the room. It was a mediocre toss. She caught it like Larry Fitzgerald, reaching high, one-handed.

I looked at the beer a little longer, closed the fridge, began pacing, front to back. It was a detective's tactic to make it look like I was thinking. I tried to do that, too.

"Awfully well-targeted attack," I said. "And did you notice how Lasko had all the posse members behind the crowd?"

"I did."

"What else did you notice?"

"The barricades were farther back from the senator than I would have expected."

She'd noticed the same things I had. No surprise. Sam was a noticer of things, too. Especially things having to do with people. Like many journalists, she'd come to the profession with a degree outside the field, in this case a Master's in psychology. Most people didn't know that about Sam. She's learned not to flaunt it, since people would then tend to treat her questions like a psychoanalysis. It was a lot easer to get answers by just being a reporter.

"And nobody but the assistant was anywhere near Jackie Brand," she said.

"Almost like Lasko expected the drone."

"Almost."

"What's Otto have to say?"

"The usual bullshit." She pushed her sharp chin down to her chest spoke in a Sheriff Otto voice—low, slow, gravelly and with a slight slur: "We don't know who was behind this tragic event, but my prayers go out to the senator and her family. We will pursue every clue until we find the evil person behind this. Meanwhile, I want to thank my deputies and the Pleasant town posse—they are heroes today. They contained the situation, prevented panic, tended to the senator. Blah blah blah."

"Otto hates Jackie Brand."

"In a big way. Not just over the bill to stop putting illegals in that outdoor prison. She's backing the mayor of Scottsdale for sheriff in the November election. She's built bipartisan support for him with key movers and shakers in and out of politics."

"Nobody's been able to unseat Horace Otto in, what, a century or so?"

"Six terms," Sam said. "Twenty-four years."

"Otto plays hardball."

"He's got as many enemies as he has friends," Sam said. "You're either with him or against him. And if you're against him, you better watch your back."

We'd both reported on Horace Otto intimidating mayors, journalists and other law enforcement officials. He'd had many of them investigated. Had a few arrested. Charges were invariably dropped, but elections were lost, careers ruined, reputations destroyed.

"What's the deal with Sergeant Lasko?" I asked.

"Not directly reporting to Otto. There's a couple layers between. But Lasko is known to be in Otto's inner circle. Otto owns guys at all levels of the organization. All the deputies know they have to watch what they say. If you're not an insider, you either pretend to be or you just keep your mouth shut."

"Never know when the one you're talking to is going to run to Otto and tattle."

"Exactly."

I kept pacing. Drank some water. "Think Lasko is involved in the bombing?"

"I have no clue," she said.

"That's my line."

"You can have it back. It's not helpful."

"Wish I needed it," I said. "Only thing I don't have a clue about right now is when I'll get another case."

"You could work on this one."

"*Pro bono?*"

"Sure. You're suspicious of Lasko. You know about drones. Sheriff doesn't seem to have any leads. You're good at figuring things out. This is what you do now."

"I don't do *pro bono*." I pretended to have a bad taste in my mouth.

"Right. You charged Delores Bernstein a dollar to find her husband's killer."

"Clients like to be sure it's a business relationship. Anyway, I think at the very least I should have a client before I take a case. I go vigilante and I'll get a reputation. It's not what I want to be. Could end up losing my license."

"There's that."

I stopped pacing and sat in the client chair. Solo came over to me, sat and stared. Solo was really good at four things. Three of them were sleeping, sitting and staring. Looking at him now you wouldn't know he was even better at attacking, scaring the shit out of a bad guy, and taking him down with just enough force to get the job done, and maybe a little more.

"Learn anything about the drone?"

"Nothing you didn't figure," Sam said. "Sheriff's spokesman confirmed it was a quad, wouldn't say what type."

"Did enough of it survive to provide any clues?"

"He wouldn't say."

"Autopilot? GPS?"

"Wouldn't say."

"Not much to go on," I said.

"Almost nothing."

Solo's head was on a swivel, listening to us. I scratched his head and he closed his eyes.

"Still, there's only so many people could've pulled this off," I said.

"And even fewer who would've."

"So we could go looking for people who know how to pilot drones."

"Where? The drone store?"

"Desert Drone Club," I said. "They fly over at the Cave Buttes Recreational Area off Cave Creek Road near Jomax Road. Bunch of DIY types mostly, pretty serious. That's where Pauly taught me how to fly one. Or there's ADU."

"ADU?"

"Arizona Drone University."

"You're kidding," she said.

"I'm not. It's a flight school. Teach you how. You get a

pilot training certificate, which these days isn't a bad career move. Department of Defense is hiring. So are police and sheriffs. Remote recon, remote bombings, crazy stuff."

"Legal bombings," she pointed out.

"Sure. Afghanistan, Syria. Anywhere the American public won't get squeamish."

"And you think you'll just go out there and find your perp."

"Probably not at ADU—a guy would have to be pretty stupid to go to school, be on record, get a certificate so he could assassinate a state senator. More likely I find someone interesting at the drone club, or somebody who knows somebody. It's informal. Guys give you tips on where to get the equipment, what to buy, how to make a drone lighter, faster, all that."

"And Pauly's there," she said.

"A lot."

"And he knows about drones."

"More than anybody else I know. So these guys learn from each other, drink a few beers together, spend a lot of time out there. They like to show off their equipment and their flying skills."

"Exciting stuff."

"Well, that's just it. Friends, neighbors, wives—they all get tired of drones pretty quickly. The enthusiasts gravitate to their own kind. Even the loners and the oddballs, and there are a lot of them."

"Which were you?"

"None of the above. I got tired of it, too. Point is, these guys know their stuff, and they know each other. They have competitions. They travel around to races. They read the magazines, surf the web sites, know the best drone flyers around the country. So our bad guy might've been out there a time or two. Or somebody there might've heard something."

"Might've," she said.

"I suppose the sheriff will think of that."

"I suppose," she said.

I pondered some more and neither of us talked for a minute. Not feeling obligated to fill a void in conversation was one of the good things we shared. No pressure. No rush.

"Quinn?"

"Yeah."

I was rubbing Solo's head, watching his eyes open and close with pleasure. If he were a cat, he'd have been purring. I felt Sam looking at me. I looked up. Took a deep breath. She smiled, then let it fade with a sigh. Whatever she was going to say wasn't going to be said now. I had a good idea what it was. Part of me wished she'd say it. Part of me didn't.

"I gotta get back to the paper," she said finally, looking away. "Zee wants to have a big news meeting, brainstorm some angles on this."

Nick Zee, the managing editor of *The Arizona Republic*. I nodded.

"You're itching to do something," she said.

"I guess so."

"You'll have a case soon. I can feel it."

I nodded.

"You'll be OK?" she asked.

"I'll be fine." I found myself nodding again and stopped. That was enough nodding for today.

Sam stood. Solo stood. Sam put her laptop in her bag. She came around from behind the desk. I kept staring at where she'd been sitting. I wanted to do something other than sit there and look at the chair. Sam bent down and let Solo lick her face. Then she turned to leave. She paused, put her hand on my shoulder, squeezed it. We didn't say goodbye. The bells clanged and the door closed behind her.

"Damn," I said.

Solo looked at me, looked at the door, looked back at

me.

"Not that simple, pal. Wish it was."

CHAPTER 4

I n the backyard with my second Sierra Nevada, I lit two pages of crumpled newspaper under some mesquite charcoal in the starter chimney. The desert sky was wide. Pinnacle Peak rose abruptly to the northeast, glowing orange with blocky shadows painted by the sinking sun. It was still hot but tolerable.

I took a long pull on the beer and soaked up the view. It was hard not to think of Jess this time of the evening, our favorite. My mind drifted quickly to Sam. Usually my mind drifted the other way, from Sam to Jess. Progress. Even mulling how my mind was muddled about all this made me feel guilty. But less so now. Trying to move on from Jess. Not succeeding yet, but trying.

The mountain faded to purple, went colorless.

By the time the charcoal was ready, three beers were gone. I felt good, yet knew I'd had enough to drink. I cooked two steaks for four minutes on each side, took them inside, cut the unseasoned steak in half. Solo sprang up and followed me back out. The half steak went in his dish. Solo sat rigid. He waited for the command to eat, and then he did, voraciously.

Back inside I opened a bottle of wine to go with the steak, a nice merlot from California with complex flavors I couldn't put names to. Solo had water with his.

"Latvia," I asked Alex Trebek, who had answered "Estonia, Lithuania." Category: "Geographic Trios." The contestants had to wait for Trebek to finish the answer before they could ask, so I beat them on this one, as I often did. Easy one. I drank some wine to congratulate myself anyway.

I wondered if Sam was watching *Jeopardy*. It was among the few shows we both liked that wasn't a comedy or detective show, or both. We were going through past seasons of *Leverage* and *Psych* again, sometimes together and sometimes separately, in sequence and in tandem.

"What is Mount Whitney?" I said to the TV. Alex had answered, "The tallest peak in the contiguous United States." Category: "Big and Tall."

The steak was perfect, medium rare. Sautéed zucchini on the side. I rinsed the dishes, went back outside with the wine glass and the bottle, sat and put my feet up on the flagstone rim of the fire pit that wasn't lit, and tried not to think.

That didn't work.

Jess had picked out the chairs. Her hands were in the plants, the trees. She was in every room.

I let myself think of Sam. The opposite of Jess. Jess never did anything without thinking and planning. She had lists for everything. She was almost always in a good, level mood, but she stressed about the little things in life, stuff that to me didn't seem stress-worthy. Our relationship had been waning, and before we figured out what was wrong, she was gone.

Sam was prone to dark moods. She could flare in an instant. She lived in the present. She dismissed the little things. And our relationship was waxing, as much as I could stand to let it. I admitted to myself for the first time that I loved them both, in totally different ways.

The night grew black, dotted by stars above and porch lights down here. The bottle of wine was more than half gone. I dozed off in the chair thinking about the case I didn't have.

CHAPTER 5

I parked the Jeep in front of Lulu's Grind. It was already eighty-seven degrees an hour after sunrise. My head throbbed lightly, my brain full of cotton. I desperately needed some of Lulu's coffee.

Beach sat at his usual table on the patio out front, squeezing a red rubber ball in his left hand. He was in his tan posse outfit, shorts and short-sleeve button up shirt, a black belt weighed down with all manner of posse things you could use to shoot, stun, club or otherwise apprehend someone with.

Beach had called early, woke me up. "Breakfast, Lulu's, soon as you can," was all he'd said, and hung up.

"Morning, Beach."

"Sit," my friend said.

I looked around. Solo was in the Jeep, already sitting. I gestured his way.

"Talking to you," Beach said. "Sit down. I don't have much time."

Beach was always straightforward, but he was never rude. This morning his tone was, shall we say, urgent. I sat.

Lulu came out and walked up to the table. Beach leaned

his chair back against the wall, watched the occasional car navigate the circle and continue up or down Pleasant Way.

"Quinn, what you drinkin' this morning?"

"Gin and tonic?" My voice was raspy and deep. I cleared my throat.

"I get you coffee."

"Thanks Lulu. And good morning."

"Oh, you in cheery mood. Good, good. Not like friend here." She pointed at Beach. "He a grump today."

Lulu smiled wide. She was from Tanzania, had been here many years. She was above average height for a woman, thin. Hair cropped short. I didn't know many women as sexy as Lulu. I didn't have a clue how old she was. Nobody knew. Her skin was smooth, wrinkle-free, but something about her—wisdom emanating from her eyes and smile—suggested she was older than she looked. I'd never seen her in a bad mood.

"People get cranky when they get to be his age," I said, pointing my thumb at Beach. "Don't let him rub off on you."

"No, no." Lulu laughed. "No grumpy old man get me down. Coffee, come right up."

Normally Beach would watch Lulu walk away. It was quite a sight. He didn't this time.

"Talk to me," I said.

"This whole thing stinks like a pig in heat." He tossed the ball over to his right hand, recommenced squeezing it.

"I caught a whiff yesterday," I said.

"Biggest crime in Arizona since Gabby Giffords was shot down in Tucson, and Sheriff Otto's treating this like a damn traffic violation."

"You're not serious."

Beach gave an audible humph. "Something's not right," he said. "I mean, I don't expect him to ask me to investigate this…"

"You being just posse."

"…but none of Otto's people interviewed me or any of the other posse."

"You figure if Otto wants the complete picture, somebody would interview you."

"Would interview every one of us. Everybody saw things from a different angle. Maybe they wouldn't learn anything they didn't get from the deputies, but that's a no-brainer, interview any lawman that sees something like that."

"Why you telling me?"

"You're a private detective, aren't you?"

"Says so on my license."

"So detect."

I squinted. Lulu arrived with the coffee. I thanked her profusely. It was almost too hot. I sipped carefully and watched my friend. Beach had already cleared my head some. The coffee cleared it a bit more. I had given up trying to figure out what was in the coffee. Lulu called it a Tanzanian tribal secret. People from other towns drove past their own Starbucks and came to Pleasant for a cup of Lulu's coffee. There was only one kind. It was simply called Lulu's coffee. She didn't make espresso, cappuccino, or any other foo-foo variations.

Lulu asked what we wanted for breakfast. Beach ordered a Denver omelet, which wasn't on the menu, but Lulu always made it for him. I ordered two scrambled eggs, hash browns, bacon, and a cream-cheese-and-raspberry pastry called Just Pleasant. Hangovers required all this. And Lulu's pastries were incredible.

"I can't just start working on the case," I said after Lulu left. "I don't have a client."

"I'm your client," Beach said.

"You want to hire me to investigate Sheriff Horace Otto. Your boss."

"Can't officially hire you, no. And I didn't say investigate Otto. I just don't see anyone else trying very hard to get to the bottom of this. Otto says he's bringing full attention to the investigation. Ha. Maybe there's a bunch of investigating going on that I'm not privy to, but my posse sense tells me there's something screwy happening, or not happening. I'm not saying Otto is behind it."

"Your posse sense?"

"Like Spidey sense. We lawmen all have it. You wouldn't understand."

Jack Beachum made me smile more than just about anyone. Not more than Sam. Not more than Jess had back when things were good. But he was a solid third. And he was a good man, a good lawman, and he always shot straight, no matter the consequences. Great friend. My best friend. Though we never verbalized that. Didn't have to.

"What's got you up on your high horse?"

"This is my town," Beach said. "Someone tries to kill a state senator in Pleasant and gets away with it, town won't feel safe."

"Lasko seemed awfully calm yesterday," I said.

Beach shrugged.

"You think he's involved? Think he tried to kill a senator?"

"Not a fan of Lasko," he said. "He's an ass. That don't make him an assassin. Bottom line, I'm just saying somebody needs to find out what the hell is going on, who tried to kill Jackie Brand. I figure you're desperate for work, so I might as well toss you a bone."

"Not sure I can work for free." I already knew I would, despite telling Sam I couldn't work *pro bono*. It was always this way—on Wall Street, at the newspaper, and apparently now as a private eye. I'd see a problem, or an opportunity, or just a challenge. I'd circle around it, determine if it was interesting and if it was a nut I could crack. Then I'd decide quickly, go or no-go, and not look back. I was just toying with my friend now.

Beach pulled his wallet from his hip pocket, took out a dollar, handed it to me. "There, you're employed," he said.

"Just don't tell anyone who you're working for."

"Otto would fire you in a heartbeat, he knew you asked me to do this."

"I'm a damn volunteer for the posse. I make sure cars don't plow through school crosswalks. I see something, I call for backup. I'm on the support crew. He can't fire me. He can only stop letting me volunteer."

***

Lulu brought breakfast. I dug in. Beach told me what else he'd gleaned, which was mostly what I had figured myself or learned from Sam.

"Did the footage from the TV crews show anything interesting?" I asked.

"Nothing we didn't see with our eyes. Less, actually. They were all trained on the senator and barely even caught the blur before the explosion."

Beach stopped talking. Squeezed the rubber ball more vigorously. He was looking over my shoulder, down Pleasant Way.

"Don't turn around," he said.

I didn't.

"Shiny black BMW just pulled into the Horny Bull."

"A little early for a steak," I said.

"The Bull doesn't open until eleven."

"Not many BMWs in the Horny Bull parking lot most days," I said.

"Pickup trucks and Harleys."

"Who's driving?"

"Can't see. Tinted windows."

"What're they doing?"

"Car's just sitting there."

"They watching us?"

"Be my bet." Beach squeezed the rubber ball so hard I thought it would pop. He continued to stare over my shoulder. "What else you wanna know?"

"What about the helicopter footage?"

"It showed the direction the thing came from." Beach pointed up and to the southwest, sighting his finger over Ringo the cactus and the roof of Café Amir just beyond the traffic circle. Scraps of plywood were still strewn around the base of Ringo. "But they were zeroed in, too, so they caught just the last bit before it came over the roof there. Just a little more than what you and I saw."

"It came straight in, no turns captured in that footage?"

"Actually made a turn toward the north just after the helicopters picked it up," he said. "Was headed due east, then northeast."

"Precisely those compass points, or roughly?"

Beach chewed. "Precisely.".

"Any idea whether it was being piloted, or if it was on autopilot?"

He set his fork down. Swallowed. Looked at me. "The guts of the drone were destroyed, so there's no way to tell, I hear. Don't know how you'd tell."

"If it was auto," I said, "there'd be more brains onboard."

"Brains?"

"A computer chip more powerful than the basic setup you need to fly one of these things yourself. Enough brains so it can get from Point A to Point B on its own."

"I know the military has drones like that," Beach said. "And deputies are using them for recon down at the border. Even Sheriff Otto has one. Privacy advocates not happy about it. So a civilian can get hold of a drone that'll do all that?"

"Welcome to the modern world, old man. You can build one or buy one these days. At a university in Europe, they released an autopilot system on a chip a few years ago, about the size of a quarter. It's got a processor similar to what you'd find in a smartphone, plus GPS, an altimeter, gyroscope, accelerometer. Runs on software called Paparazzi, developed more than a decade ago specifically for autopiloting UAVs, or what we now usually call drones. The software was pretty glitchy early on, but it's a lot better now. Both the hardware and the software are open source."

"Which means?"

"Which means anyone can use it, develop it further, improve it."

Beach interrupted me. "He's moving."

His eyes followed the BMW around the traffic circle.

"Act natural and keep talking."

I leaned back in my chair, put my hands behind my head, laced my fingers together.

"How's this?"

"Almost looks natural," he said.

"You gonna shoot him?"

"Not just yet."

"Get a license number?"

"Nope. Too far." The rubber ball nearly exploded as it bounced off the patio and back to Beach's hand. Then the squeezing again.

"Want me to look?"

"My eyesight is fine," Beach said. "Cataracts, remember? They gave me new eyeballs. I'm twenty-twenty again. See better than you, by my bet. There. He's gone."

"OK good. No more acting."

"As an actor," Beach said, "you're a pretty good detective. Where were we?"

"Paparazzi software and chips," I said. "At least one company is making and selling the chip now. But any company could. Practically speaking, an individual would have to buy one of the chips. Other companies sell all the same stuff in kits or pre-assembled. The end result is bigger and heavier, not all on one chip, but this isn't new technology at all."

"So the inventors are giving away everything you need to

build and fly a drone on autopilot, do exactly what happened yesterday to Jackie Brand, and companies are selling these things fully assembled and ready to kill."

"That's probably not their intention," I said. "But basically, yes. Although you have to add your own bomb."

"Holy mother." Beach tossed the rubber ball back and forth between hands. "Seems like a lot of potential for bad things to happen."

"That's what they said about the internet back in the nineties," I said.

"And for the most part they were right."

I shrugged in partial agreement. "Technology can be used for good or bad. Drone proponents figure someday guys like you, and firefighters, will all have drones in your pockets."

"Just another tool," he said.

"Like flashlights and radios."

"Or guns," Beach said. "Speaking of which . . ."

"Not going to happen."

"Quinn, you got lucky the first time. Either of those guys—the big Slav or Bobby G or that idiot Johnson—could've popped you."

"None did. And I wasn't lucky. I was careful. And skilled."

"Goddamn karate. Won't stop a bullet."

"Taekwondo."

"Yeah, whatever. Your judo shit got you out of a couple jams last time. A gun would've worked just fine and been safer."

"Or I might've killed someone," I said.

"Someone might've deserved it."

"But I didn't need a gun. I don't need a gun. I don't want a gun. Just enough force . . ."

"And maybe a little more."

"Maybe a little more."

"Gotta admit," Beach said, "I kind of enjoyed what you

did to Earl Johnson. Anyway, what do these chip setups cost?"

"The autopilot hardware and software, generally a few hundred dollars."

"And the drones?"

"Good entry-level drone costs just a few hundred. I would guess the one we saw yesterday was a lot more than that, but this isn't as expensive as buying a car."

"These things even legal?"

"You're the posse member."

"Haven't run across any situations." Beach took the last bite of his omelet, slid his plate away. "Until yesterday."

"All drones, commercial or private, are supposed to be registered with the FAA. Other rules covering how and where they can be used are emerging, so it's a little confusing, but suffice it to say, it's illegal to blow people up with one."

Lulu brought more coffee and the bill. I reached for it but Beach snatched it away. It was a game we always played, and we never argued over who would pay. Over time it evened out. He gave Lulu his credit card and watched her walk away. He wasn't strong enough to resist that twice in one day. I kept my eyes on Beach.

"So what if this thing wasn't on autopilot?"

"You could still have targeted the senator," I said. "But it'd be harder to do it so precisely, if you weren't within sight of the target. You could tell the thing to fly perfectly east, turn to the northeast, and it would do so. A good remote pilot could do that, I suppose. Maybe even dive it down and slam it into the podium. You'd use the drone's onboard live video to guide you, if you knew where you were going and were familiar with the area. Would've taken a good amount of know-how and skill either way. But I'm guessing autopilot."

"Why?"

"That also saves a guy having to stand nearby to run the

controls, and look obvious," I said. "One of us—me, you, a whole damn posse—might have noticed someone piloting that thing."

"Unless he was hiding."

"Yeah. Wouldn't rule that out. But if I wanted to pull off what we saw yesterday, I'd go with autopilot. Wouldn't be anywhere near the scene. Plus it allows for advance planning—if you know where the target will be, you just program in the GPS coordinates and a route."

"How would you know where the target is gonna be?"

"Indeed," I said.

"Yeah, noodle that."

My bacon, eggs and hash browns done, I took a bite of the pastry. I held up a finger to let Beach know there would be no talking during this first delicious bite. I had some ideas on the targeting. Didn't share them yet. It was sometimes good to noodle with someone, it was sometimes good to noodle alone. Right now I wanted to have some more facts, maybe even a lead, to noodle with. I set the pastry down, swallowed, drank some coffee.

"You said security was tight," I said. "How tight?"

"We had the entrance to town blocked off hours before the speech. Nobody came in without showing ID or being a local."

"You blocked the town entrance?"

"Easy to do here."

"One way in, one way out," I said.

"Be stupid not to take advantage of that."

"What about after?"

"Nobody got out the rest of the day without showing ID. We asked a lot of questions."

"You harassed them."

"We questioned them vigorously."

"See if they get nervous."

"Yessirree."

"And?"

"Unless one of the good citizens of Pleasant has gone rogue and pulled off an Academy Award performance, I don't think the bomber slipped past us."

"Autopilot," I said.

"Be my guess, too."

"Any chance I can get a copy of that helicopter footage?"

"That'd be against regulations." Beach leaned back, scrunched eyebrows and pursed lips looking all serious. "Might get me fired."

"Any chance I can get a copy of that helicopter footage?"

Beach reached into a backpack under his chair, pulled out an unmarked DVD in a thin plastic sleeve and slid it across the table. "Butch Cassidy and the Sundance Kid," he said. "Ever seen it?"

"Only four or five times."

"Great ending. You should watch it again."

"Thanks," I said. "I owe you one."

"I've lost count."

CHAPTER 6

I jogged out of Pleasant and turned south on Pima Road, stayed on the left shoulder to keep an eye on oncoming cars and bikers. The sky was wide open, unbroken blue. Heat rose in waves off the pavement.

The plan was for six miles in forty-two minutes, give or take fifteen seconds. I checked my time at the large mesquite tree, my one-mile mark: 7:30. Perfect warm-up mile. I'd run the other five in 6:50 to 6:55 each. I quickened my pace.

My mind moved from focusing on the running to thinking about my second case.

With pinpoint accuracy, a drone had slammed into Jackie Brand's podium. The senator had been well separated from the crowd and the posse. From my days as a reporter, I'd learned to be suspicious of anomalies, especially when it came to politics, big business or the law. The setup yesterday didn't look normal.

Meanwhile, with few solid facts and no real clues, I applied wild-guess percentages to some possibilities, leaving room for other likelihoods. It was an imprecise but useful tactic for zeroing in an elusive truth.

Odds of this being an assassination attempt: ninety-nine percent. Hard to imagine anyone but Brand was the intended target.

Likelihood the drone was on autopilot: eighty percent.

Chances the pilot, or whoever programmed the drone, was highly skilled: ninety-five percent, leaving room for luck. I could not have pulled off what I saw yesterday without some serious honing of my skills, and probably some help.

I drank some water from a tube connected to a pack on my back. Felt the heat and sweat. Smiled at the efficiency of muscles and joints and chemicals churned out by the brain, giving me the natural high that was just settling in.

Increasingly I thought there might have been a homing device on the senator, in the microphone, or somewhere under the podium. That would've simplified the targeting. And it would mean someone involved in setting up the event had helped. Or one of the deputies or posse members. Or Sergeant Lasko. I didn't know enough to put percentages on any of this yet, but my brain blurted some out anyway.

Seventy percent chance that more than one person was involved in the assassination attempt. Sixty-forty someone was on the inside, part of the setup team or law enforcement. Fifty-fifty it was Lasko.

Odds were probably higher on Lasko. But I needed some evidence before those odds could be raised. Reason and intellect can deduce truths, or so the theory of rationalism goes. The downside of rationalism is that you can be one-hundred percent convinced of something and, on closer examination, find out you were dead wrong.

But in the absence of a smoking gun, or even much of the smoking drone, or hardly any evidence at all, I had only rationalism to move the investigation forward, so I embraced it warily, just as I'd often done as a reporter.

Two miles in. Checked my form. Elbows in. Hands relaxed. Strides efficient. This southern trek on Pima Road was slightly downhill, as Pinnacle Peak and the rest of the mountains of the North Valley gave way to Scottsdale and the broader Phoenix Metro Area, so it was easier than the return leg would be. The sky was still blue, without blemish, the air still dry and hot. I put my body back on autopilot.

Earlier I'd gone back to the office and watched the video of the drone taken from the TV helicopter. Just as Beach had said, the drone came in from the west.

From above, the drone could be seen heading perfectly eastward, parallel to the roof lines, just south of Tranquil Trail. The drone was mostly a blur in the video, but I could make out its shape, confirming four rotors. As it approached Pleasant Way, it jogged at a forty-five-degree angle and flew northeast over Café Amir and directly toward the podium on the east side of the central circle, in front of Ringo the cactus.

I'd grabbed an old-fashioned printed map of Pleasant from the bookshelf. Used a ruler and pencil to draw a line from the site of the explosion to the center of the roof over Café Amir. Then westward. There was no way to tell if the drone had made other turns along the way. But if you were programming a drone to go from point A to point B, it would make sense to fly it in one direction until it was close to its target, then adjust for the final stretch. Not the only way to do things, but the logical way. Odds: seventy-thirty. Something to go on. A lead. Might point toward a clue.

I hadn't deciphered anything new, but I'd organized my thoughts, and that's all I needed to work out for now.

Ahead, a familiar boulder off to the side of the road. Three-mile mark. My breathing was light and even. I'd keep the same pace on the return leg but have to work harder to do it. Glanced at my watch: 20:54. Right on schedule. Turned, crossed the street, headed home.

My brain was empty for a moment, then it pictured Sam. I shook my head to get her out of it and focus on the run. Didn't work.

CHAPTER 7

My iPhone was ringing when I stepped out of the shower. I dried my hands and found Beach on the other end.

"Beach, twice in one day. You must be lonely."

"You find anything out yet?"

"Nothing."

"When you gonna start detecting?"

"You only put me on the case a couple hours ago," I pointed out.

"Lazy ass. Listen, I got a tip. But." He paused.

"But?"

"I'm not sure if I should tell you."

"We both know you're going to."

"If anyone finds out . . ."

"Beach, you been giving me tips since way before I became a detective."

"You were a good reporter."

"I was a great reporter. And I never let on that you helped me. Mum's the word. You know that."

"Just be extra careful with this. Don't use it to try and stir anything. Don't be obvious."

"On Lincoln's Bible."

"They found something."

"They who?"

"The team investigating the scene. Not sure exactly who."

"What'd they find?"

"Official word is it was just part of the loudspeaker system."

"But."

Beach lowered his voice. "Guy I know at HQ says there's a rumor it was a homing device. Figures it was supposed to get destroyed, so whoever put it there didn't expect anyone to find it."

"But someone did. And that would explain the accuracy of the strike."

"And it means . . ."

"Somebody on the inside is involved."

"You bet your ass it does."

"But it's just a rumor," I said.

"And if Otto or one of his inner circle guys wants to make it go away, that's all it'll ever be."

"Why do you think they'd do that?"

"Bad publicity, at the least," Beach said. "If that's it, they'll try to find the guy, fire him for some other reason, make it all go away quietly."

"And not worry whether they solve the case."

"Otto's got no love for Jackie Brand."

"Yes, I keep getting reminded of that."

"Worst case," Beach said, "inside guy is one of his, Otto knows it, and he's covering for him. Or somebody is."

"Well, it's not likely Jackie Brand's assistant did it."

"Not likely."

"TV crews and reporters wouldn't be high on my list of suspects," I said.

"Mine neither. And I don't remember any of them being near the podium during setup. I was there most of the time."

"I'll have to find out who set it up. Third parties involved or not. Who else on Brand's staff was there before or during the event."

"Sounds like a lot of work."

"For a dollar."

"You could drop the case, give me my money back, admit defeat."

"Not a chance."

CHAPTER 8

Despite the afternoon heat, we walked. It was dry. Sweat evaporated before it could get sweaty. It was two blocks from my office, down Pleasant Way, past the central town circle to Tranquil Trail. Sam had left the paper early, showed up as I was leaving the office. Solo was between me and Sam, panting eagerly. I had the sudden urge to hold Sam's hand. I didn't try. Wondered if I ever would.

"Probably."

Sam looked at me sideways. I didn't look at her, but in my peripheral vision I saw her pull her hair behind her ear. I knew she was smiling. I realized I'd said it out loud.

"Quinn?"

Figuring I should say something, I told Sam what Beach had told me. Well, I told her some of it.

"The video from the helicopter shows the drone heading due east, over the buildings on the south side of Tranquil Trail. Then it takes a sharp turn just before it gets to Pleasant Way. You know the rest."

"Probably," she said.

I smiled.

I didn't tell Sam about the rumor of the homing device. I'd promised Beach I wouldn't mention that to anyone. Sam wasn't just anyone, but telling her about it probably wouldn't help me solve the case. Withholding something from Sam didn't feel good. But it felt right. Right wasn't always comfortable. We jaywalked across the empty street and turned right on Tranquil Trail.

"So we're going to walk west and look for clues."

"Exactly," I said.

"And what exactly are we looking for?"

"No clue," I said. "Yeah, I know. I have to stop saying that. But it's not a clue until you find it, so how can you know what it is ahead of time? Anyway, stop interrogating me. I'm supposed to ask the questions."

Sam smiled again. This time I saw it directly. Jesus, it was a helluva smile.

"I figure maybe the drone originated somewhere nearby," I said. "Was maybe set up the night before or something, programmed for the mission and waiting for a green light. The shorter the distance of the mission, the less room for detection or error. Too close and you're in the busiest part of town, risk being caught setting it up."

"The mission," Sam said. "That makes it sound like a good thing. Like a NASA voyage. Or a Navy Seal operation to rescue our guys."

"The deadly mission?"

"The senator is still alive. Christ, Quinn. You really need to work on your crime vocabulary."

"The assassination attempt."

"Now you're getting the hang of it. So how far we going to walk?"

"Don't know. Until we find something or run out of places to walk."

The center of Pleasant, the old part of town, was a grid four blocks north-south by six blocks east-west. There were just three blocks before we'd get to the edge of the old part of town and the transition to suburbia. I hoped we'd find something interesting by then. Following a straight path out through the suburban streets was impossible without hopping walls and navigating swimming pools in back yards. The streets were all giant curves, meandering to follow the contours of the desert landscape and provide a faux sense of randomness to the placement of homes. Or to simply confuse anyone passing through.

We passed the yogurt shop, the flower shop, an insurance agent, a realtor. I knew the owners of all but the yogurt shop personally, and she seemed pleasant enough. No reason to suspect any of them. But you never knew. For now, they were all suspects of low probability. That was about as useful as saying everyone was a suspect. My thoughts were spiraling beyond reason.

We crossed the next street, walked past a doctor's office, an eye doctor and a dentist. The next block marked a shift away from professional services to grittier retail. There were fewer people around. An auto repair shop, tire shop and then a bland, two-story building with dusty windows and nothing but bare walls inside. Like most buildings in the old center of Pleasant, this one was old, wood-framed. The windows were intact but the panes were prehistoric, the paint cracking and peeling, gaps where wind and dust would get in. A red and white for sale sign was taped to the inside of the window, with a phone number written in black marker. I stopped. Sam stopped. Solo stopped.

I asked Sam: "You know who owns this?"

"Nope," she said. "But it's been vacant for months. Used to be a cleaners."

I checked the doorknob. Locked. I looked up at the second floor. More dusty windows, but smaller. An apartment. I logged the phone number in memory.

Out of the corner of my eye I saw a window shade move on second floor of the building across the street. I'm not the paranoid type, but ever since I'd been jumped by the big

Slav in the Bernstein case, right in front of my own house, I paid more attention to anything unusual that might tip me off to danger. Especially when I was doing things like trying to turn locked doorknobs on abandoned buildings while looking for an assassin. I also knew better than to look up. If there was someone watching, I wouldn't want them to know I knew. If I'm going to be surprised, and I know it, I want to retain the element of counter-surprise.

Solo tensed slightly, too. I don't think he saw any curtains move. Probably sensed my tension. I tried to stay relaxed, move on to the next play.

There was a narrow passage between the building and the tire shop. A gate was meant to discourage anyone from going back there. I opened the gate and we went back there. I was pretty sure we were noticed.

Solo felt it, too. He perked his ears up and dropped his hindquarters a bit, prepared to spring forth if needed. Solo was no ordinary dog. He'd been trained by the sheriff's K-9 unit and was ready for service, except for a couple personality flaws. For one, he didn't feel the need to bark incessantly when cornering a bad guy. One bark was it for Solo, then he'd get down to business and growl in a way that'd scare the crap out of the meanest of the mean. But the training manual called for more barking. He was also a bit of a free spirit. He'd sometimes anticipate the next move before his trainer released him, such as trying to rip the arm off the pretend bad guy before he was commanded to try and rip the arm off the pretend bad guy. Two no-no's in the training manual. Solo made it all the way through school but flunked the final. While I was still getting over Jess' death, my friend Jack Beachum helped find Solo a home. Mine.

We stepped around a pile of broken shelving and rusted florescent light fixtures that'd been left behind, then around a loose stack of empty buckets and a few withered cardboard boxes. Solo looked at me, looked toward the back of the building. He seemed to know something was up. His training must have included investigations into abandoned buildings.

"What are we looking for?"

"Don't know," I whispered. But if you were going to launch a drone on an assassination attempt, wouldn't the roof of an empty building be the perfect launch pad?"

"Feels like a stretch," she whispered.

"One of the key strategies of private investigating is seeing something that feels like a stretch, and then pulling at it."

"Wouldn't it be easier to find obvious stuff to pull at?"

"I haven't seen any obvious stuff."

"And if there was some, you'd see it."

"That's why they call it obvious."

"Not everyone sees the obvious."

"But I get paid to."

"Why are we whispering?"

"Well, we're trespassing, and I don't see any reason to shout about it," I said. "That's the obvious reason."

"There's another reason?"

"I think we're being watched."

Sam just nodded. We'd worked together enough—on investigative stories at the paper, on my quest to hunt down Jess' killer, and on my first case—that we trusted each other's instincts.

At the back of the building more junk was piled on the concrete. Boxes, clear plastic garment bags, a few ragged clothes, and a mountain of wire hangers. There was a six-foot concrete block wall surrounding an area about eight feet deep and the width of the property. The buildings on either side and behind were single story.

"Private spot," Sam said.

There were two small windows on the second floor, none on the first floor. The door was nondescript, windowless. I tried to turn the knob. It wouldn't turn, but the door drifted open. Solo growled once, low and barely audible.

The jamb had been shattered. I looked at Sam. Sam looked at me. We went in. The space was cool and dark. A thin layer of dust coated the floor. What I saw there could not have been more obvious.

"Footprints," I whispered.

"First you think we're being watched. Now you see footprints. What're you, Shawn Spencer?"

"I can sense these things," I said. "Why aren't we whispering anymore?"

"Two sets of prints." She pointed them out. "One going in, one coming out. The ones coming out are farther apart, less distinct. Walked in. Ran out. Nobody's here."

"What're you, Veronica Mars?"

Solo sniffed at the first footprint. Not sure if he knew all the details, but humans are dropping dead skin cells all the time, and they leave a trail that any well-trained dog can pick up. Solo looked up at me for instructions on what to do next.

"Good boy," I said. I wasn't sure what the command was for "see if you can sniff out clues to a potential assassin who might've come in here with a drone," so I said: "Keep your nose open."

"Keep your nose open?"

I shrugged.

"Should we report the break-in?" Sam was thinking clearly.

"The building has been empty for more than a year. Anyone planning to burgle the place could clearly see from the street that there's nothing to steal. Footprints seem to be pretty fresh. Whatever happened here, I doubt it was a theft."

"Still, maybe the sheriff should know."

"Sheriff already knows plenty," I said.

"Meaning?"

"I don't think the sheriff is going to work very hard on

this case."

"How do you know that?"

"I can't say. Sorry. I know something but I can't tell you."

"Confidential source."

"Right."

"Beach?"

"Can't say," I said. "Confidential source."

But Sam knew. That was OK. Sam wouldn't get me or Beach in trouble. Now she knew enough to understand why we should not report the break-in, and I hadn't told her the thing I'd sworn not to.

I pulled my iPhone from its holster and took photos of the footprints. I was not a footprint expert, and I didn't know any footprint experts, and these didn't strike me as unusual footprints in any way, but as a private investigator, it seemed like the smart thing to do. We followed the footprints across the floor to the stairs on the far side, followed them up. The stairs creaked a bit, ended on a small landing with a door. Solo sniffed the doorknob, growled a bit. It was unlocked. We went in.

The apartment was not dusty, but whoever had broken in left a couple dusty footprints heading toward another stairway that led to an interior landing and the roof. Solo sniffed the floor and headed straight for the stairs, so we followed.

I read somewhere that I had about five million olfactory receptors in my nose and Solo had 225 million. I let him continue to do the sniffing.

The stairs were narrow. We went up single file. At the small landing was a narrow wooden door leading out to the flat roof. The door faced south. Solo sniffed the doorknob, growled a little louder. It was unlocked, too, so I opened it and we followed Solo out onto a small wooden deck that covered the back portion of the roof.

Solo started sniffing again, went in circles a few times,

growled, then sat down and looked at me.

"Good boy?" I said.

Solo barked. Just once. I didn't know what he knew, but I knew he knew something.

"Great view," Sam said.

You could see in all directions, across the one- and two-story rooftops of the old town center and beyond to the suburban homes that surrounded old town. The sun was getting low in the west. The view to the south was unobstructed, with no other two-story buildings in the line of sight. The landscape slid away to the south, through Scottsdale and Phoenix. In the far distance, enveloped in slight haze, the mountains just beyond Baseline Road marked the southernmost border of the Valley of the Sun.

Around the perimeter of the roof was a parapet maybe two feet high. If you stayed low, nobody could see you up here.

I told Solo to stay, and of course he did. Sam and I stepped to the side of the structure that enclosed the landing. I looked and pointed to the northeast, purposely not looking directly at the second-story window across the street, due north, but this time I definitely saw movement. A person, big blond hair, black clothing that billowed a bit, maybe a dress, probably a woman, moved out of view behind the curtains. Pinnacle Peak towered behind the building with the mystery snoop. My peripheral vision was pretty good.

"Look where I'm pointing. We are being watched by Curtain Woman. Act natural."

"You got it, Columbo. Curtain Woman?"

"Don't look. Second story across the street." I was still pointing. Too much pointing. I moved my hand to shade my eyes, instead. Put my other hand on my hip. The classic "I'm not looking at you, I'm just acting casual" look. "That the roof of Café Amir?" I nodded my chin toward it.

"Looks like it," Sam said. "I've never seen it from here.

But that's where it should be."

Café Amir and the other two-story buildings blocked any view of the central traffic circle, just more than two blocks away. But we had our bearings, the lay of the land.

"Short distance as the crow flies," Sam said.

"Or a drone."

She put her hand on my back. It felt good. Very good. Maybe too good. As close as Sam and I had become, I suddenly realized that touching wasn't something we'd done yet.

"Just acting natural," she said. "We're talking a lot, acting a little stiff, and it probably looks like we're pretending not to try and figure out who Curtain Woman is. If she is watching, we don't want her to think we're spying on her, too."

She laughed, for no reason, and punched my shoulder. That didn't feel so good.

"Pretty private up here," she said, swinging her arms and looking around as if we were considering buying the place. "If you come out the door and stay crouched, nobody would see you. Stay behind the landing and you can stand up without being spotted."

"And whoever is watching us probably knows that."

"Good place to do something nefarious from," she said.

"Like make an assassination attempt."

Solo was still sitting in the same spot. Waiting for us to do something. I didn't know what to do, but there was nothing more to see here, so I said "C'mon, boy," and we left.

CHAPTER 9

The sun had just risen above the mountains to the east. The air was still. Pleasant was bustling with traffic for a Saturday. I stuck the key in the door of my office but found it unlocked. I knew I'd locked it yesterday afternoon when Sam and I left to follow the path of the drone.

My body tensed. I wished I'd brought Solo with me. Since I didn't carry a gun, I had two primary means of protection: Solo, no explanation needed, and my own hands, which could hurt a man faster than he could say "Hey, what the." Correction: could kill a man. Not that I ever wanted to. But it was good to know they could.

Still, there were a lot of people around, on the sidewalks, going in and out of the cafes. A clutch of Harleys was parked in front of Lulu's Grind. A small line of mountain bikes shushed past, heading north on Pleasant Way toward the trailhead. Not a good time to commit a crime, so if somebody broke in, it was probably overnight, and it was probably over.

I was overthinking all this. After taking an instant to clear my head and focus, ready for anything, I pushed the door open and went in.

Unless he'd been sitting there all night, the rough-looking pile of muscle sitting in my Aeron chair had recently committed the crime of breaking and entering. His feet were up on my desk.

I closed the door, kept my hands ready at my sides, moved into the room casually but quickly to get away from the wall, knees imperceptibly bent and ready.

"You're sitting in my chair," I said.

"My chair right now."

The pile of muscle showed his perfect white teeth. He was shorter than me, probably five-eleven or so. Thick everywhere—jaw, neck, arms, chest. Weightlifter. Strong but slow, I hoped. Not likely to be a problem if we ended up tussling, as long as I didn't let him get close. But you never knew. Skin smooth and dark but with wrinkles starting to form, maybe late forties, maybe Italian, a little too much time in the sun. Black suit, gold chain that screamed tough guy from Jersey, black Reebok walking shoes. Slender hands folded across a flat stomach, fingers manicured.

"We'll fix that shortly," I said.

He ran his left hand through his gelled black hair, as if it needed to be put back in place.

"Listen, asshole," he said. "Nobody's moving me until I wanna move. Anyway, I don't plan to be here long. Unless you want to go at it right now. Then I'll have a nasty mess I have to clean up, and that'll take a while. Neither of us wants that."

"So you're the thug," I said. I decided to think of him as Tough Guy No. 1, in case there were more as I continued pulling at the strings that seemed attached to the assassination attempt on Jackie Brand. I wasn't expecting to get his name, so I figured it best to start keeping track somehow. "How about you just tell me what I'm not supposed to do, then you can leave and I'll go do it anyway, and we'll be done here."

"Wise ass."

"So I've heard."

"Listen, asshole. I know who you are. Eli Quinn, private fucking detective."

"Says so on the sign outside. Except for the fucking. So now we know you can read. Or at least sort of. And you can pick locks. The surprises are piling up."

"And I know what you've been up to."

"I call it snooping around. What do you call it?"

"I call it *asking for it*," he said. He ran his left hand through his hair again, removed his feet from my desk, stood up. Tried to make himself taller than he was. Five-ten was all he could muster, with hair. Maybe five-nine without. Being a pile of muscle, however, he seemed bigger. I had a good reach advantage on him. That always helped.

"You been visiting places you shouldn't," he said. "That shit stops now."

I wanted to ask if he knew Curtain Lady. Kept that to myself. But I didn't want to miss the opportunity to shake the tree a little and see what bad apples might fall, now that Tough Guy No. 1 had confirmed I'd found the tree. "If I don't snoop around, how am I going to find the guy who flew that drone?"

Tough Guy No. 1 didn't blink, didn't give me anything. He might not know much. Sometimes the Tough Guy is nothing more than that, and he doesn't need to know why. But I was pretty sure whatever I said would get back to whoever had sent him.

"Let's keep this simple, asshole. I know where you work. I know where you live. I know where you're not supposed to be. Knock this shit off right now, you and I won't see each other again. Keep it up, you're fucked. Somebody gonna be scraping pieces of you off the floor."

"Duly noted," I said. "Appropriately terrified. Otto send you?"

Nothing. Tough Guy No. 1 was good at sticking to his

script. Or he didn't know what the heck I was talking about. Good odds both were true.

"Wise ass," he said. He moved around the desk, didn't bother keeping eye contact as he headed for the door. That was the sort of lapse in focus that would've been my opportunity, were I looking for one. I had him beat on smarts, reach and focus. And I was pretty sure I had him beat on fighting technique. By a mile. His shoulder bumped mine to make it clear nobody gets in his way. I didn't bounce out of the way, as he expected. But I didn't press the issue by bouncing him out of the way, either. Just establishing some reasonable boundaries. He was looking for an excuse to fight. I was not.

Tough Guy No. 1 paused at the door, turned, flashed his perfect white teeth again. "I do hope we see each other soon," he said, crossing his arms and gripping his left bicep with his right hand. "It'd be fun."

He unfolded his arms, turned, opened the door and left.

"A blast," I said when he was gone. I was calm, but plenty of adrenaline had flowed through me, so I pulled my shoulders down, flexed my fingers, and began to relax. I'd been in situations like this before, situations that could go either way, might not end pretty, lots of testosterone on both sides. I wasn't getting used to it. I'd never get used to it. That'd be dangerous. But I knew how to handle it. And I knew what I'd do next.

CHAPTER 10

Nobody would accuse a Jeep Wrangler of driving itself. You had to wrestle the steering, jam the gears, drive the damn thing, on-road or off. I'd never heard anyone complain.

South on Cave Creek Road, right on Jomax into Cave Buttes Recreational Area, then I took a right and manhandled the Jeep across a disappointingly smooth dirt road that led to the Desert Drone Club. Solo was in the back, smiling in the breeze we made on an otherwise windless morning. Good day for flying. It would be hot soon, but it was still early and the temperature was enjoyable.

The lot was nearly full. I parked the Jeep a ways from the small clubhouse, beyond which several drones soared, hovered, dipped, flipped and generally filled the sky.

Solo and I walked over. The clubhouse was small, low ceiling, noisy fan in the middle of the room, no air conditioning. A few mismatched chairs faced a small TV on the wall. There was a kitchenette, stacks of boxes of bottled water on the counter. Two guys grabbed donuts from a box and a bottle of water each and went out the back door.

Another guy came in the same door and went to the restroom.

Paul E. Peters was sitting in a worn club chair watching open-wheel sprint car racing on the TV. I recognized him from behind. Grey cargo shorts, black Teva sandals and a navy blue polo shirt. Sandy blond hair curled round his ears and flopped over his forehead. He was slouched in the chair, legs in a man spread, drinking a Bud.

"Pauly, it's not even nine o'clock."

"I know. Amazing. With cable you can watch racing twenty-four-seven." He glanced at me, tipped his beer my way, then looked back at the television. "I don't get this channel at home, so I figure what the hell."

"Janet must miss you."

"Probably doesn't even know I'm gone." He looked at his watch. "It's Saturday. She's still snoring. Kids probably watching that crap on the Disney channel or playing World of Warcraft." He turned in his chair partway to face me. "So anyway, where the hell you been, Quinn? It's been what, a year? You're a lousy freaking friend, you know that?"

Last time I saw Pauly was at Jess' funeral. More than a year ago. Neither of us wanted to bring that up.

"Yeah, time flies," I said.

"Around here it just drones on."

"You told me that one before."

"Still funny."

"Hilarious."

Pauly Peters got up. It took some effort. He was six-six and weighed about two-forty. Not fat, just big boned and solid. Though he was putting on a little around the middle lately. Pauly and I were best friends in college, roomed together our first year in the dorms, played some intramural basketball, drank a lot of beer and shot a lot of pool. We took different paths after college but stayed in touch over the years, then found ourselves both in Arizona. We had the kind of friendship that didn't need much tending. We could go a year without even talking, and pick right up as though we'd been hanging out every weekend.

Pauly was a hard core gamer, built his own gaming PCs, was a hell of a power forward who always threw an elbow to draw a foul in the first minute and screw with the head of the other team's big man. And he could run the table in eight-ball. He worked for the CIA and almost never talked about his job. Even I didn't know exactly what he did. Just that it was classified, involved brains not brawn, that he sometimes went away for weeks to faraway places and couldn't say where, that Fortune 500 companies had him on speed dial, and that otherwise he seemed to have a lot of spare time. And he knew more about drones than just about anyone.

"Good lookin' mutt," Pauly said.

Solo stayed by my side. He took his time warming up to strangers.

"Paul E. Peters, meet Solo. Solo, this is one of the few tough guys you'll meet who I *don't* want you to attack."

"Trained to kill?"

"Not exactly," I said. "Subdue with force."

"Looks like a killer." Pauly put his hands in the air, fingers spread, made a face like he was afraid.

"Sometimes he uses just a little more force than necessary. But mostly he's well disciplined, and friendly, long as you don't do anything stupid."

I put my hand out. Pauly grabbed it, then pulled me into a hug and we gave each other a good slap on the back. Solo didn't attack.

"So what brings you here?"

"I'm looking for someone who knows a lot about flying drones," I said.

"You're talkin' to him."

"Someone else," I said.

"I thought you quit drones."

"I did. But I'm looking into the strike on Jackie Brand

day before yesterday."

Pauly raised his right hand, flew it down into his left palm with a waist-high smack. "Dead on target. Somebody knew what they were doing."

"Yep."

"You're back at the paper then?"

"Nope."

"So you're just curious?"

"I'm a private investigator now."

"No shit. Hell." Pauly rubbed his chin, nodded. "Eli Quinn, private eye. Makes perfect sense. You were always figuring stuff out. So you're working for the sheriff?"

"Nope. Can we talk privately?"

Another guy came in the front door, grunted good morning. The guy in the restroom came out and headed for the donuts.

"C'mon," Pauly said. "Let's walk."

At the back door he pointed to an open guest book on a table.

"Gotta sign in. Put me down as member. Print and sign your name."

"Just to take a walk?"

"Rules is rules. No reason not to follow them."

I signed in and we went out.

Twenty or so guys were spread out around the edges of a broad, flat, bare expanse of desert, each with a controller in his hands, neck craned skyward. Drones buzzed every which way, a flock of mechanical ravens on caffeine. A faint whir of rotors. The ground was all dirt and rock, a few weeds that were fading with the summer heat.

"Talk to me," Pauly said.

"Between us."

"Sure."

"Totally between us," I said, looking him in the eye.

"C'mon, Quinn. You know you can trust me. I'm with the CIA."

"Yeah, about that. *Totally* between us, OK?"

"On my mother's grave," he said. He put his hand to his heart.

"Your mother is fine."

"Scout's honor?" He saluted me with his left hand.

"Here's what I think," I said. "The drone was on autopilot. Probably had a bead on exactly where to go. Was set up beforehand and then somehow activated remotely. Or maybe activated manually but then autopiloted to the target. Whoever sent it on its way couldn't see the target. Flew two or three blocks. Pinpoint accuracy."

"Homing device?"

"I didn't say that. And if you inferred it, you didn't infer it from me. And you need to forget you inferred it. I got someone to protect. Way better friend than you. You talk about this to anyone, my friend is toast."

Pauly nodded. I trusted him. I had to. "Homing device," he said. "That's how I'd do it. And from what you describe, sounds like that's probably how your assassin did it. But now that I think about it, I can't remember what we were just talking about."

"Thanks Pauly. Failed assassin, by the way. At least for now. Brand is in a coma."

"How sure are you of all that?"

"Hundred percent on the coma. The rest is a working hypothesis, but a damn good one. I shook the tree a bit, and some bad apples are starting to fall out and confirm the hypothesis."

"Odds?"

Pauly's mind worked like mine. I thought for a moment. All the odds I'd placed on the various scenarios just yesterday were pretty iffy. But I'd learned a good amount since.

"Ninety percent on the general idea," I said. "Maybe eighty-twenty on the details."

"How can I help?"

"I'm looking for someone who could do what I just described."

"Half the guys out here could do it." Pauly swept his hand across the stark landscape.

"I'm looking for someone who *would* do what I just described."

He pulled his arm in, cupped his hands as if holding something small, shrugged his shoulders. "Probably a smaller number."

"You think of anyone with those skills who might've passed through here, maybe not a regular, maybe seemed suspicious somehow?"

"Hell, Quinn. I think everyone is suspicious. It's what I do."

"Anyone in particular?"

"Not off the top of my head. But I'll think on it."

"Maybe poke around? Discreetly?"

He stopped walking, put hands on hips. Followed a drone that was corkscrewing through the sky. "I could do that."

"Thanks Pauly."

We turned around and walked back to the clubhouse. I asked about his wife.

"Janet's good. She says I spend too much time out here. Should do more around the house, in the yard. Hell, we have someone who cleans the house once a week. We have a landscaper, comes once a month. And we have nothing but cacti and a couple trees in the yard. What am I supposed to do?"

I had introduced Pauly and Janet in college, was best man at their wedding. And despite the way he talked sometimes, I knew he was still nuts about her and the kids. And somehow she still put up with him. It made me think of Jess. Then Sam. Pauly had met Sam a couple times. I told him how she'd been the one to suggest I become a private investigator, and how she'd handed me my first case—the

Bernstein murder. How she'd even helped me solve it.

"You and Sam spending a lot of time together."

I wanted to tell my old friend about what was really going on with Sam. But I wasn't even sure what it was, so I just nodded.

"She's about the most beautiful a woman I've ever seen," Pauly said. "And real. Nothing made up or put on."

I nodded. No questioning any of that.

"Strong headed."

I nodded with more enthusiasm.

"Smart as hell."

My neck was getting tired.

We shook hands in the clubhouse. Pauly was glancing at the race on TV—there were ten laps to go. Steve Kinser, the oldest guy in the race by a decade, was in third, but half a lap off the lead.

"He'll never get there," I said.

"Lots of left turns to go," Pauly said.

He was back in the club chair before Solo and I were out the door.

CHAPTER 11

I'd stopped at the hardware store and bought a hole saw for the drill and a deadbolt for the front door. Instead of a keyed lock I got one with a smart lock to operate with an iPhone app. Next time someone wanted to break into my office, they'd have to actually *break* in. The instructions were awful. Which is to say, I wasn't as handy as I'd like to be. I had the lock installed but couldn't get the deadbolt to fit right with the new slot I'd carved out crudely in the jamb.

Solo was curled up on his dog bed in the corner. No help at all. I was chipping away at the jamb with a hammer and a small chisel when my phone beeped and vibrated. I pulled it from the holster and was surprised to see who it was.

"Got some names for you," Pauly said.

"That was quick."

"I hear the first couple days are the most important in any investigation. So anyway, assumed you'd want me to get right on it."

"How'd Kinser do?"

"Tapped the guy in front of him and spun the guy out, got a solid second."

"Not bad for an old guy."

"Amazing."

"So what have you got?"

"The Desert Drone Club keeps records on its members. Just basic info, but we know who belongs and pays dues, address, phone number. I was able to hack in and have a look, then I did some analysis on the names."

"Analysis."

"None of your business."

"Gotcha."

"So anyway, I've got two names that might interest you."

"Go ahead."

"Frank Colangelo. I know him pretty well. He's an ace drone pilot, has built more flying machines than even me. Turns out he's got a record. Something about embezzlement in Jersey. But it was a decade ago, and it looks like he moved to Arizona, made a clean start. He sells insurance down in Tempe.

"None of that exactly makes him an assassin," I said.

"Nope. But it's a red flag. Other guy is Michael Derbin Smith. I only know him a little. Doesn't like to be called Mike or Mikey."

"He's probably our guy, then."

"I doubt it. He's not really the DIY type. Buys out-of-the-box drones. Not all that bright, probably couldn't have designed or built the setup you describe. But he hangs out here a lot, likes to fly tricks. Not good enough to win any competitions, but he has fun trying."

"So why'd you flag him?"

"Smith is the shifty type, kind of an asshole really. I'd always kept an eye on him, just because that's something I can't *not* do. But I didn't have any reason to do more than that. Anyway, turns out he's been in and out of county jail for a slew of mostly minor offenses, from shoplifting to resisting arrest."

"Sounds like the Desert Drone Club needs to vet its

applicants."

"Yeah, right? I try to stay out of the politics around here, but I might suggest that now. So anyway, I know about Brand's stance on immigration and her standoff with Sheriff Otto over the outdoor prison. That got anything to do with all this, you think?"

"Crossed my mind," I said.

"Figured. So anyway, Mikey Smith is white trash. He and I don't talk much, other than a hello here and there, but he talks plenty to others. Disparages Mexicans. *Send them all back, build a wall, arrest every last one of them*, crap like that. He's not the only one in the club like that. I mean, this is Arizona. Lotta guys like that. But he's the loudest and the stupidest."

"So that makes him a person of interest," I said. "Interesting but probably not capable."

"Yeah. But that's what I got. I have a couple other names, even less likely."

He gave me those and I jotted them down.

"I didn't look at the guest list, since it would take a while to paw through, and there's no phone numbers or addresses on the guests, so no easy way to run them."

"This is a big help."

"All yours from here. But hey, these guys might be clean, so look into them quietly. Especially Colangelo. No need to start rumors about him if he didn't do anything, and he probably didn't."

"Of course. Thanks Pauly."

I clicked the phone off and holstered it. Opened the laptop on my desk and launched the browser, typed in Frank Colangelo. There were forty-four Frank Colangelos at Whitepages.com, a slew of them on Facebook, a dozen on LinkedIn, and pictures of a whole bunch of them. I added Tempe to the search query and found *the* Frank Colangelo. He had a robust profile in social media, but nothing that screamed "I would try to kill a state senator." I bookmarked a couple pages for later.

I searched Michael Derbin Smith. There was only one. Multiple mug shots, a few small news stories of his various arrests. I clicked on his Facebook page. Not exactly family friendly. If you were looking for clues to Michael Derbin Smith's stand on immigration, his Facebook page would serve as a position paper.

I read through some of his posts. Mikey was busy on Facebook. Lots of commentary on news stories from the past few days, local stories and beyond. Much of it poorly written. Some of it incoherent. Most of it inflammatory. He railed on Muslims, Mexicans and even Canadians (for being weak on immigration and letting terrorists cross into the US). Links to right-wing opinion pieces railing on the lack of border control in the nation and in Arizona, all interspersed with off-the-cuff complaints. *Saw a dozen illegals at Dunkin Donuts this morning waiting for jobs. Our jobs. Send them home!* Lower down: *If the cops would just shoot them the jails wouldn't be so full.* Then: *McDonalds shouldn't serve anyone who can't speak English!!!*

Plenty to move Mikey officially from my persons-of-interest list to my list of suspects, especially since I didn't have much of a list yet—Tough Guy No. 1 on the first list and Sergeant Lasko on the other, and pretty much no evidence on either of them.

I scrolled back a couple days.

Then Mikey did what so many ideologues do, because they just can't help themselves. He put a big fat clue on his Facebook page. A great big glaring clue that was just sitting there shouting *I did it* or at least *I wish I'd done it.*

Being an ace detective, I spotted it.

The clue was a comment and a link to an article on the American Border Containment website. The ABC was one of the most virulent anti-immigration groups in the country. It was based in southern Arizona. Mikey's post read: *ABC awfully happy about Jackie Brand!*

He didn't say *should be happy* or *might be happy*. He implied that he knew they *were happy*. I considered that Michael Derbin Smith might've just gotten his wording wrong. Muddling his meaning with words was something he was actually good at. But still.

I surfed around the American Border Containment website to refresh my memory on their stance. At the top of the home page was a quote from the founder, Ted McCall.

Illegal immigrants are invading our country. A cancer is spreading from our southern border and it is infecting every state in this great nation. We must kill the cancer, stop the spread. Join today and help us fight the foreign invasion.

Fairly clear stance.

I scanned some more, then read an article about the ABC from the Southern Poverty Law Center, a civil rights group that highlighted hate and aimed to stop it. In a nutshell, American Border Containment's activities ranged from lobbying for anti-immigration legislation to helping fund and conduct vigilante border patrols. They held rallies, produced incendiary videos, and recruited like-minded people to join in activities and fund their efforts. Several of their members also belonged to various white supremacist groups.

I followed some links to learn more about Ted McCall. State champion wrestler in high school, unremarkable but winning record as a middleweight boxer in his twenties. From his pictures I gathered he was late forties now, tightly cropped graying hair, fit and rough-looking, like an Irish fisherman you would not want to mess with in a bar. These facts weren't relevant for now, but I logged them in memory anyway. If Ted McCall was to become a suspect, it was good to know who I was up against.

I read on. McCall had long been associated with multiple hate groups. He formed ABC in the late nineties. For years it was a relatively obscure group, but lately it had tapped into increasing anti-immigrant sentiment and become a more vocal and visible group. I'd seen McCall on television a few times. He was like Michael Derbin Smith but in shape and with an education and a vocabulary.

I wondered where Ted McCall had been the last few days and what he'd been up to.

CHAPTER 12

Sam picked up on the first ring. I put the hammer and chisel down again. Pulled some bits of wood out of the hole in the jamb, grabbed the phone from between my ear and shoulder.

"You still hot for that FBI guy?"

"Screw you," she said. "I told you he's just an old friend." She paused. I waited. "What's up," she said, an edge to her voice.

"I got a name," I said. "Ted McCall."

"The ABC leader."

"Right."

"He's the bullying type. Asshole, first rate. Confrontational, provocative, sometimes right at the edge of the law. But he's never killed anyone.

"That we know of," I said.

"Fair enough. It's a short hop from bully to much worse disorders. You like him for Jackie Brand?"

"Don't know," I said. "But I might have connected him to a small-time anti-immigrant creep who likes to fly drones and who posted something interesting on his Facebook page."

I told her about what Pauly had told me, about Michael Derbin Smith and his Facebook post about American Border Containment.

"How's Pauly?"

"He's good. Same old Pauly. He asked about you."

"And what did you tell him?"

I didn't have a good answer to that. So I didn't answer. Sam let the lack of an answer hang there. Payback for the FBI-guy comment.

"This Smith guy said *ABC's awfully happy*?"

"Yep," I said.

"Not *should be happy*."

"Nope."

"Interesting."

"Yep."

"So what's your next move?"

"I was hoping you'd help me figure that out."

"What's the job pay?"

"Less than a dollar."

"Perks?"

"Dinner?"

"What can I do for you, Detective Quinn?"

"I was hoping your FBI friend might know somebody who knows somebody who keeps an eye on guys like Ted McCall. I'd like to know where he is, go talk to him. Better, I'd like to know where he's been the last few days."

"My friend is on the FBI's Art Theft Crime Team."

"But he might know somebody."

"Might. And I can call some other contacts. I've written some stories about ABC, know some people who know a lot about them, and about their fearless leader."

"And I'd love to know if McCall and Smith know each other. And I'm really curious if McCall knows how to build and fly drones."

"I'll look into it."

"Sam?"

"Quinn."

"Thank you. I know you don't have to help. I've been leaning on you a lot."

"I like it when you lean."

I smiled and clicked the phone off.

The leads and clues were piling up, and I thought about what I should do next. I could go at Mikey, but first I wanted to know if he and McCall had a relationship. If not, everything I'd learned today might go nowhere. And I wanted to know where to find McCall. I knew he had a home in southern Arizona, near the border in Nogales. I hoped I wouldn't have to drive down there. I also knew he spent a fair amount of time here in the Valley, getting himself on television, rubbing elbows with state politicians, doing who knows what else. Would be good to know where he stayed when he was here, and where he was now, and where he was the day of the drone strike. Either way, I was pretty sure I'd be paying a visit to McCall, Mikey or both.

And I wondered how Sergeant Lasko might fit into all this. Maybe not at all. But my suspect list was growing.

I twisted the deadbolt. Surprisingly, it slid smoothly into the jamb.

CHAPTER 13

When I needed to think about something without actually thinking about it, I either went for a run or came to Choi's Martial Arts. I parked in front of Master Choi's dojo, two blocks south of Tranquil Trail and not far from the building where I figured the drone had been launched.

Inside the high-ceilinged industrial space it was cool. The last class of the day had just ended and kids swarmed the small, spare entrance lobby, grabbing shoes and gear bags and threading their way out. I put my shoes in a cubby, bowed and stepped onto the red and blue mat.

Twenty minutes of warm-ups worked up a good sweat, but I hadn't forced the Jackie Brand case into my subconscious yet. The facts and names and faces and questions were all still swirling around at the surface. After my warm-up I figured I'd kick the bag some then lift weights in the back. Somewhere during all that I need to stop thinking about all the things I was cogitating on, see what my mind turned up when it wasn't focused on the case.

The dojo had emptied and only Master Choi was left,

sitting on a stool in the corner, quiet.

"We spar," he said.

I was surprised. Master Choi sparred at half-speed with the kids regularly, and sometimes with some of the adults who were working their way up through the color belts. But in his mid-fifties now, he rarely sparred with me or the other adult black belts. When he did, it was so he could teach something, rather than being competitive. He might set up a kick to the head and then tease you with what could have been, but he never put his full force or skill into the sparring. I'd long wondered what he was capable of.

I nodded with a slight bow. We put on our pads. Sparring hurt enough with the chest protector. Without it, either of us could easily break the other's ribs.

"Not see you much since you become private detective."

"It's been busier than I expected. I just got another case."

"Always make time," he said. "Taekwondo not part-time job. Is life."

"I know, Master Choi. I know. I'm sorry."

In the years I had been with him, Master Choi had helped me improve all my hand positions, moves and kicks, quickness and power. He'd taught me focus and control. And he'd taught me how to hurt and subdue or even kill. "Never use if not need," he always said of these moves. "Run first. Defend second. Fight last."

"You not get fifth-degree belt," he said now. "Been two years. You close. Now you go backward. You not practice. Two years take four years. No focus. Chasing girl. Getting in fights."

Master Choi was talking about Sam. He didn't know her, but he thought of her as a distraction. I wasn't exactly chasing her, but I didn't want to try and explain that. And he was talking about the guys I'd roughed up during my first case.

"I told you, I only defended myself," I said.

"You try run?"

"They had guns. Running might have gotten me killed."

"Next time run. Taekwondo last resort. Not like movies. Respect skills. Respect master. No more fighting. Now we spar."

Not wishing to disrespect my master, I kept my mouth shut. The confidence of taekwondo could keep me out of a fight. But sometimes it got me into one, and I was OK with that.

We went to the middle of the mat. I bowed deeply. Master Choi bowed less deeply, being my master.

We squared off.

"*Seijak*," he said.

We began circling each other. Master Choi attacked quickly, stepped in with a roundhouse kick and then spun and caught me in the side of the ribs with a back spinning hook kick that nearly knocked the wind out of me. I should have blocked it but his swift aggression caught me by surprise.

I thought I'd known Master Choi's style well. He preferred patience and counterattacks. Though he was a head shorter and several years older, he had just reminded me that he had vastly more skill and experience.

I reset my stance, got up on the balls of my feet and started moving. Master Choi was smiling now.

"Focus!" he said, tapping the side of his head with a gloved hand.

I circled him, stepping in sharply but drawing back. I lunged with an ax kick. He backed up and I struck air. I moved in, went airborne and executed a good double roundhouse kick. He blocked the first but the second delivered to his mid-section, weakly. As my second foot touched the ground I'd left my chest open and Master Choi struck quickly with a push kick. Not terribly forceful but enough to knock me off balance. Master Choi stepped in to show me what he could've done to an off-balance opponent, then he withdrew. I was beaten, but he let the lesson continue.

And so it went for another five minutes. I landed a few kicks, no punches. My opponent never let me get close enough for a punch. I was in good shape. Very good shape. But I was out of breath. My ribs would be sore. My ego was bruised. The message was clear. And just to be sure, Master Choi repeated it.

"You not focus," he said, tapping the side of his head again. "Taekwondo only get you hurt if you not focus."

He returned to the center of the mat and we faced each other.

"*Kyung nae*," he said.

We both kept our eyes on each other as we bowed.

CHAPTER 14

Amir Yalda made the best baba ghanoush on the planet. Mine was a close second. Even Sam admitted that. She was stunning in a simple black dress with a thick silver chain necklace and no-nonsense flats. Sam didn't need more than three things to dress to the nines.

The night air was warm, low-nineties still. Most of the patrons at Café Amir ate inside. We were on the patio, looking across the traffic circle at the intersection of Pleasant Way and Happy Lane. Ringo the saguaro stood sentry. Beyond Ringo on the northeast corner was Lulu's Grind, and a block north sat my new office.

I finished my glass of wine and poured another. Sam had barely touched hers.

"It's a small town," I said, staring out across the traffic circle and not looking at Sam.

"That's what we like about it."

"But we like New York, too."

"We do," she said.

"We've never been there together."

"We haven't," she said.

"How long were you there?"

"Two years at NYU. I lived at the Y. Awful place, but it was home. I hung on for another couple years waitressing and trying to find my way. Would've stayed but when I finally got a job it was in Indiana. Which led to Arizona."

"Would've been interesting if we had met in New York."

"I wouldn't have liked you," Sam said flatly.

I looked at her, raised an eyebrow.

"You were Wall Street. I was living in the Y. I was idealistic, maybe a little naïve, but full of hopes and dreams.

"And distrustful of Wall Street."

"Totally. I wouldn't have given you the time of day."

"I'm still the same guy."

"No you're not."

She was right. I felt like the same person in many ways, but when I looked back at the me on Wall Street, I barely recognized him. I definitely didn't miss him. I was glad he'd invested wisely, so I could do what I was doing now.

I asked: "You ever think of moving back?"

"Tough place to live. Rent is outrageous. Winters suck."

"But if you've got money, a decent place…"

"The culture," she said. "I miss the culture, the diversity, the noise, the bustle."

"I miss it all," I said. "But I do love this town. This spot. This weather, this night."

Sam nodded. I stopped there. I wondered what would happen if one of us left Pleasant. Would the other follow? Outwardly, we were just friends. But it was rapidly becoming much more. And if we acknowledged what it was becoming, then at some point we'd be thinking about our future together. I hadn't thought about my future since the moment I learned that Jess had been killed. I'd been living in the past and the present, mostly wallowing in it. Chasing down Jess' killer. Waiting for his trial. Watching him get convicted. Deciding not to go back to my job at the paper. Deciding to become a private detective, renting an office and renovating it, then finally taking a case, sort of. Every move, every decision, in the moment, no consideration for tomorrow. And every step of the way, Sam was there.

"You have a future here," she said. Seeing into my thoughts again.

"And a case to solve," I said.

"About that."

The waitress brought our dinner. We both leaned back and let her put everything down. I had the chicken shawarma with rice. Sam had only side orders, which she'd promised to share with me: tzatziki, grape leaves, hummus, and of course the baba ghanoush.

"No tabbouleh?"

"Gets stuck in my teeth," she said. "Remember?"

"Vanity."

"Practicality."

"Yeah." I asked her what she'd learned.

"You know about the vigilante patrols at the border," she said.

"Militia-style methods, tactical gear, AK-47s. Rising violence, especially lately."

"Right. It's gotten so bad, agencies like the BLM have been doing security training with their employees. Sheriff deputies have had guns pointed at them. The militants are targeting immigrants and drug trafficking, but they've become so dogmatic, everybody seems to be their enemy."

"Our Ted McCall hasn't been involved in any of this, I don't suppose."

"McCall may not be the angel we thought," Sam said. "Going back to the late nineties, I found several instances of vigilantes shooting immigrants at or near the border. Three of them stood out over the years. Two immigrants were killed in the first one, one in the second, and in the other, three people were injured, no deaths. There were other cases like these, but these three had something in common."

"Ted McCall the shooter?"

"Not officially, no."

"Meaning?"

"McCall was a suspect in these cases, but the charges were dropped each time. I studied some other cases, and there were others in which the charges were dropped, but some at least went to court, and there's been a couple convictions."

"You think McCall has someone looking after him," I said.

"Might."

My second glass of wine was gone so I poured another. Sam's glass was half empty so I filled it. I looked at the empty bottle and wondered if I'd order another. Knew I shouldn't.

"What else?"

"Oh, this gets good," she said. "Your friend Michael Derbin Smith? He was on patrol in all three of those shootings."

"Mikey and McCall together. Hmm. That sounds like an authentic lead to pursue."

"I think so," Sam said.

"How would you characterize McCall?"

"Dirtbag."

"Is that your professional opinion?"

"Ah. No. That would be antisocial personality disorder."

"In English?"

"Psychopath or sociopath," Sam said. "I don't know enough about him to say which."

***

Sam sipped her wine while I pulled my phone out and called Pauly.

"I got a name for you."

"Lay it on me," Pauly said.

"Ted McCall."

"That asshole? What about him?"

"Can you see if he's ever been out to the club?"

"Guest list is analogue, my friend. Paper. Might take a couple hours."

"You there now?"

"Am."

"Doing anything?"

"Am not."

"Then can you hop to it?"

"Will."

I clicked off.

"Any idea where McCall is these days?"

"That wasn't so easy," Sam said. "You're going to owe me more than dinner for this."

She paused. I waited. She smiled thinly. I tried to act cool. Her smile broadened knowingly and her eyes sparkled with mischief, and she continued.

"He's got the big horse ranch down near Nogales. And he has a smaller ranch in the foothills outside Black Canyon City, just up the 17. It's in the name of someone he's known to associate with, but he spends a lot of time there, and the, ah, well, some people know it's really his. He has a few horses, but otherwise the ranch house just sits on a bunch of empty acres. Not a lot of activity that anyone has noticed. So you were right: The law is keeping an eye on him, but only half an eye."

"Which law?"

"If I tell you that I'd have to kill you," she said.

"Keeping secrets from me?"

"And you don't keep any from me?"

I smiled. We ate a bit. I drank my wine.

"You're hunky FBI friend help you with this?"

"Stop it," she said.

"It's not the sheriff, is it? The sheriff isn't worried about McCall."

"I can't say," Sam said. She looked at me a little sideways. It was a hint.

"Feds," I said.

"I didn't say that," she said.

"I hear you," I said. "What else you got."

"McCall isn't physically tailed. They're not watching him every step of the way. But they keep tabs on his whereabouts."

"Let me guess."

"Yep. He's been in Black Canyon City the past week."

"Aha." I tried to look and sound impressed. And I was.

"And Mikey?"

"Lives in a trailer park off I-17 near the 101."

That was in Phoenix, north side, a fifteen-minute drive west of Pleasant. She handed me a piece of notepad paper with Mikey's address on one side and a simple map to McCall's ranch on the other. I looked at both sides.

"So that's what, thirty minutes from Mikey's trailer park to Black Canyon City?"

"At most."

"Interesting."

"At least."

***

I was sitting in the backyard looking at the stars, having a gin and tonic I didn't need, when Pauly called, got right to the point.

"Ted McCall was indeed a guest of Michael Derbin Smith a few months ago."

"Bingo. You know what they did?"

"I asked around. Sounds like McCall did a little flying, was a very good pilot. He mostly kept to himself, stayed close to Mikey. But one of the guys said he asked about autopilot software and hardware."

"Double bingo."

"I don't think that's a thing. But yeah, in my line of work we'd call that a big freaking clue. You're welcome. So anyway, I didn't press for details, wanted to keep the conversation casual since you asked me to be discreet. I can root around some more if you want, maybe rattle some cages."

"No thanks," I said. "I'll do the rattling. I don't want you to get your hands any dirtier than they are now."

"I appreciate that."

"Thanks Pauly."

CHAPTER 15

Not all trailer parks in Arizona were run down. Many were surprisingly inviting, well landscaped, with palm trees and well-paved streets. Snowbirds flocked to Arizona in the winter to escape the lousy weather of the northern states and Canada. Most of them were not filthy rich, and the trailer parks, some with essentially permanent structures and some packed with motor homes that were driven down and back, offered a relatively inexpensive solution for a second home. Many were tight communities where like-minded people got to know their neighbors, enjoy their retirement years.

Michael Derbin Smith's trailer park was none of the above. It was a hot, squalid, noisy patch of dirt and blacktop next to I-17, sandwiched between a U-Haul center and a place that rented cranes, backhoes and other construction equipment. There were no palm trees. The homes, most of them essentially permanent structures, were faded, sagging, rusted.

Mikey's place was white and turquoise blue, colors you'd expect on a boat, not a house. A faded dark blue Toyota Corolla, hubcaps missing, paint rendered splotchy by years of relentless desert sun, sat in the drive.

I decided to keep our first meeting direct, short and sweet. I was pretty sure Mikey was not a kingpin of anything, but I was almost certain that anything I said to him would get back to some other people, and I knew from experience that would probably start a chain reaction that would lead to someone getting back to me. Might be Tough Guy No. 1, might be Tough Guy No. 2, who I hadn't met yet, or maybe Ted McCall himself. Regardless, if my theory was even close to being right, Mikey was the string to pull that would start the whole ball of mystery unraveling.

It was five-thirty in the morning. The sun had just risen. Surprise visits were best conducted during regular sleeping hours. Bright mornings tended to be safer than the middle of the night—less chance of me getting shot. Even better, the sun was at my back. The things you learn as an investigative reporter.

Solo hopped out of the Jeep and stayed at my side. I wondered if Smith's scent was in Solo's nasal registry.

I put one foot on the first of two rickety wooden steps and rapped three times with my knuckles on the plastic window of a thin metal door.

Nothing.

I pounded louder, four times with the side of my fist. That got a reaction.

"The fuck!"

I waited. Nothing. Pounded again and stepped back.

The door swung open, slammed against the side of the humble abode. Thin man, average height, nondescript brown hair over the ears, two-day shadow on his face, white t-shirt and red boxers. He scratched his crotch, squinted into the early morning sun. The smell of propane and day-old garbage hit my nostrils.

"Mikey. You look awful. Worse than your mug shots."

"Who the fuck are you?"

Solo growled almost imperceptibly. No bark. Michael

Derbin Smith had not been in the building off Tranquil Way where the drone may have been launched, but he was quickly putting himself on Solo's watch list.

"Eli Quinn, private detective." I handed him a card. He didn't take it.

"Big fucking deal. Nobody calls me Mikey. And I ain't done nothing."

"Here's the thing, Mikey. I'm liking you for the Jackie Brand murder." That wasn't true, but I wanted to see how he reacted. Smith looked suddenly wide awake. As with his ill-advised Facebook post, he'd tipped his hand.

"Don't know no Jackie Brand."

"Really? Mikey, Mikey, Mikey."

"Don't fucking call me that!"

Solo growled a little louder. Mikey looked at Solo, as if he'd just noticed him. I watched the fear rise in his eyes, the way things dawn slowly on cartoon characters that've just run off a cliff but haven't fallen yet.

"I was checking out your Facebook page just yesterday. Could've sworn I saw you post something about the senator. In fact you seemed pretty pleased that somebody tried to kill her."

That quieted him down. He narrowed his eyes, trying to get a better look at me. The sun behind me made it difficult.

"Who flew the drone, Mikey? You or Ted?"

He paused a telling beat. Then: "Don't know what the fuck you're talking about."

He stepped forward and reached for the door. It was an awkward move, since the door was still wide open and against the side of the trailer, the handle out of his reach. I reached over and grabbed the door, swung it around partway. He reached out for the knob and I swung it just out of his reach. Now I was just screwing with him for the fun of it. He almost tumbled down the stairs but caught himself.

"Mikey, you don't want to talk, that's fine. But things are

going to get difficult for you real soon. You help me, I might be able to help you."

"Go fuck yourself."

"That's not very helpful."

He just glared at me. I had what I needed, and I'd done what I came to do. I flicked my card at his feet and it landed on the floor inside the trailer. I wanted him to have it so he wouldn't mess up my name when he ran to Ted McCall with his news. He just kept glaring at me.

"You change your mind and want to help, just give me a call."

CHAPTER 16

The bells on my office door clanged. Solo hopped to action quickly from his mid-morning nap but stayed on his bed, standing, hindquarters low and ready, probably letting me know that Tough Guy No. 1 or 2 was about to walk through the door.

The aviator sunglasses preceded the man. Sergeant Lasko. That was quick. I'd had that nice chat with Michael Derbin Smith not two hours ago. My list of prime suspects was rounding out nicely.

Lasko stepped in, closed the door, folded his arms. His muscles were still bulging, face even more stone-like than when I'd seen him last.

Solo didn't bark, didn't growl, but he gave Lasko a mean look. It was the same as his friendly look but with his tongue in his mouth.

"Piece of shit dog you got there," Lasko said, tilting his head toward Solo. "Rejected from the K-9s, right?"

"I hear he didn't like the company."

"Couldn't pass the test, what happened."

"Chose not to follow the rules," I said. "All that barking. Ain't no dog got time for that."

I had my feet up on my desk, hands behind my head. It was one of my favorite thinking positions. I stayed that way. It was also a good position for looking fearless. I'd read in a detective novel once, never show the other guy you might be frightened. Even a little. Even if you might be. Especially if you are. I added those last couple parts. Try as I might, fear was a sensation I could not will away. It was something to manage. Feet up, fingers laced behind my head. Fearless looking.

"Dog comes at me, I shoot him, see?"

"Dog look like he's coming at you?"

"Looks ready."

"That's what I pay him for. Lasko, right?"

"Sergeant Lasko."

"That's what I meant."

"Don't wise ass me. You got a detective license?"

I pointed with my thumb at the framed license on the wall behind me. Laced my fingers behind my head again. We were a sight. Me kicked back and calm. Well, appearing to be calm. Him with arms crossed, sunglasses on indoors, looking tough as nails. And he probably was. Two tough guys not giving an inch. A real Western standoff. I hoped there wouldn't be a shootout. Seriously, I really hoped there wouldn't be.

"Detective go sticking his nose where it don't belong could lose his license real quick," Lasko said.

"Quickly," I said.

I saw his eyebrows furrow just above his sunglasses. He didn't know what to make of that.

"You think you know shit," he said. "You don't. So I'm gonna make this real simple, see? You put your nose back where it belongs, or I will."

"Mr. Lasko..."

"Sergeant."

"Lasko, you've got a nice shiny badge, representing an institution I respect greatly. And despite your odd penchant for sounding like a forties gangster, I'll do my best to give you whatever respect you deserve. But I'm still trying to figure out how much that is."

"Quinn, right?"

"Detective Quinn. Not Sergeant yet. Working on it."

"Wiseass *fuckhead* Quinn." He glared at me a second. Actually he just kept glaring. "I'm watching you," he said. He actually did the two-fingers-to-his-sunglasses-to-me thing. Solo growled. Lasko's head moved ever so slightly as he looked over at the dog. "Here's the deal. You're officially obstructing justice lately. And I can get you for trespassing, I need to."

"Curtain Lady tattle on me?"

No reaction.

"Mikey Smith call you?"

Nothing.

I was going to invoke Ted McCall, but I'd pushed enough buttons. He knew enough now to do something stupid, but not enough to do something smart.

"You don't know what the fuck you're doing, Quinn. I'm gonna let you off with a warning for now. But you get the hell away from whatever you think you're chasing, right now today, or I swear I'll hang you by your balls. I'm the kinda guy shoots first and thinks later, and I got my finger on the trigger, see?"

I wasn't sure exactly how I'd meet my demise, but it sounded gruesome.

"That sounds like a genuine threat," I said. "So I'll respond genuinely: I know exactly which side of the law I'm on right now, and I'll continue to abide by it. I'd advise you do the same. That includes not shooting any dogs that don't need shooting."

"Fuck with me, you're a dead man, Quinn."

He turned and walked out.

I unlaced my fingers, swung my feet to the floor, took a deep breath and made up my mind to prove him wrong.

CHAPTER 17

The speed limit on I-17 was seventy-five, but the Jeep wasn't made for speed, so I kept it at seventy as I wound through the foothills heading north. With the top down, the afternoon sun was brutal, but air at seventy miles an hour was comfortable enough.

I'd left Solo at home. He didn't like the heat so much, and I didn't know how long I'd be out in it, surveilling. The big plan was for a covert stakeout. It went like this: I'd find a spot to sit and watch the McCall place from a distance, see if I could learn anything.

A sign welcomed me to Yavapai County. No longer in the jurisdiction of Sheriff Horace Otto or Sergeant Lasko. Hmm. A few miles later I took the Black Canyon City exit, turned right on Coldwater Canyon Road into the less-populated part of the small town, and doubled back southward. I glanced at the note with Sam's directions. In a quarter mile, I turned left on Deadman's Drive. A ribbon of crumbling blacktop stretched due east, in up-and-down waves, disappearing into the mountains.

Small, squat houses sat on oversized lots. The blacktop gave way to washboarded dirt. Front yards collected old cars and trucks on blocks. I couldn't have been closer to a major city and further from modern civilization. A good place from which to conduct any manner of illicit operation.

As I came over the next rise two men were standing just off the left side of the road, talking to each other across a barbed-wire fence that enclosed an acre or so with a small home in the middle.

The man on the road side was old, tall, overweight, in jeans and a vast t-shirt. My detective's acumen suggested he hadn't walked far, probably lived in the home on the other side of the road, where a rocky driveway went up a slight incline to a modest home and then continued on up a ridge to the southeast. A rusted '56 Ford pickup sat in his driveway, its bulbous front fenders enveloping headlights like droopy eyelids. His hair was longish and wispy, sans any color or consistency, like dust gathering above his head then lolling to one side when he turned to look at me. Huge droopy eyelids matched the '56 Ford.

The other man, inside the fence, was younger, thin and curved like a delicate question mark. Long black stringy hair, crooked teeth, dressed in black from his baseball cap to his boots, with a giant skull on his t-shirt and a matching one on the cap.

They stopped talking as I drove by. Skeleton man crossed his arms. Mr. '56 probably would have if he could have.

I gave a friendly wave. It wasn't returned. They eyed me with the sort of squints reserved for strangers.

Now I wished I'd brought Solo.

Sam's map indicated a turn ahead about a hundred yards. The unmarked drive to the left disappeared quickly down into dry wash, then reappeared in the distance leading to a ranch style home whose rich browns and pale greens blended into the desert. Ted McCall's place. A glance in the rearview mirror revealed the two men by the road still watching me. A bead of sweat formed on the back of my neck and rolled under my collar.

Farther up was a fork in the road that peeled off to the right and headed up a ridge. I drove past the turnoff to McCall's place and took the fork to the right. The road quickly deteriorated into two barely visible ruts, wheel width apart. I put the Jeep in four-wheel drive and grinded it up the steep incline, groaning over some large rocks and slipping on some loose soil, but never out of control.

What was left of the road veered right to a flat spot just below and to the south of the ridge. I stopped and turned off the engine. The Jeep would not be visible from McCall's ranch house, Deadman's Drive, or anywhere but the next ridge to the south. I got out and walked the few steps north to the ridge I was on, took in an expansive view of a broad valley rimmed by mountains, a dry wash cutting through it all. From here I could see almost all of Deadman's Drive. Mr. '56 was gone. Skeleton man looked away, pretending he hadn't been still watching me.

The Jeep ticked a few times, cooling down, then went silent. I jumped when a covey of quail flushed from a nearby bush. I'm not usually jumpy. Next time I do a stakeout, Solo would have to come with, no matter the temperature.

Deadman's Drive was below. Beyond it was the ranch house, a modest interruption to an expanse of open desert. Out front was a black BMW. I wanted to pull out a notebook and write down "great big possible clue." I didn't carry a notebook.

Behind the ranch house, five horses stood under a corrugated metal roof, hanging their heads and looking bored in the afternoon heat. No other structures were visible for a mile or so beyond. Closer to me, the southwest corner of the McCall land abutted Skeleton Man's property.

I turned around and looked south. The extension of Mr. '56's driveway would've been over the next ridge, out of sight, no more than a quarter mile away. That bothered me too, but I needed to find out what the hell was going on here, and that would involve risks. I accepted the risks.

Another twenty yards up the hill and around a slight curve in the ridge, a low mesquite offered shade. I hiked up and took it. I couldn't see the spot alongside the road where the two men had been, or any of Deadman's Drive to the west of that spot. But I had shade and a good view of McCall's place without anyone there being able to spot me. I sat on a rock beneath the tree, began what I figured would be a long, hot, boring, stakeout. As it turned out, it was indeed hot.

CHAPTER 18

I'd been under the mesquite tree for twenty minutes. Nobody had come in or out. The black BMW hadn't moved. Then a nondescript, medium-sized white commercial van with no signage rumbled down Deadman's Drive and turned onto the narrow dirt road leading to Ted McCall's ranch. It was maybe twenty-four feet long, two axels, dual rear tires, the sort that delivers furniture. Dents, scratches, and black smudges marred the side panels. The van was dirty, hadn't been washed in months. If you passed it on the highway, you wouldn't give it a second thought.

The van was followed a few moments later by a white crew-cab, four-wheel-drive pickup truck. They were far enough apart so as not to appear together. That they both turned down McCall's driveway was surely not a coincidence. Sun glinted off the white van's windows, and the driver was on the far side from my perspective, so I couldn't see him. The pickup had tinted windows that revealed nothing.

The vehicles bobbed down into the dry wash, disappearing briefly and then reappearing. Dust billowed behind them.

When they got to the ranch house, the van driver made a loop in the front yard and backed the van up to the garage, turned the engine off. The driver got out and went to the back. He was average height, thin, and that's all I could determine from this distance.

The pickup pulled in. Nobody got out. The garage door swung open. I heard somebody shout in Spanish, muffled sounds riding a slight breeze to my ears. It sounded urgent. I couldn't see any detail in the shadows behind the van or inside the garage, but I could tell there was activity of some sort. Within less than a minute the garage door closed, the driver got back into the van, and the van and the pickup left.

I considered following them. It'd be hard to do without being noticed. A red jeep on a dusty, deserted, ramrod-straight road. I decided to stay under the mesquite and watch the house a while longer.

The house just sat there. I stood and stretched, kept my eye on it.

Twenty minutes later, still standing there, someone grabbed my shoulder from behind and spun me around. A fist approached at high velocity. I rocked back reflexively and the punch landed on my right cheek and eye with slightly less force than intended. Enough to knock me to the ground, but not knock me out.

I rolled back reflexively, using the momentum of the punch to execute a perfect reverse summersault, and I was on my feet, expecting to see Skeleton Man or Mr. '56, as unlikely as that might seem. It was Lasko, and he was coming at me again. I stepped to the side and his second punch missed barely. I gave him a short jab into midsection with my left hand and he grunted but didn't seem affected. He swung around and threw an elbow that caught me in the ribs, which were still sore from Master Choi pounding on them. The pain was sharp and deep, as though his elbow had gone between two ribs and into my chest cavity—but nothing seemed to be broken. I let the momentum carry me out of arm's reach, got into the ready position with knees bent, left foot forward, fists in front of me.

I breathed deeply, ignored the pain.

Lasko was in plain clothes, jeans and an army green t-shirt that stretched over freakishly large muscles and protruding veins. Same buzz cut, no sunglasses this time. His eyes were cold, pale blue, more like ice than sky. He was taller and bigger and stronger than me. I'd need to keep some distance so this didn't become a wrestling match. But he probably had a gun, so I'd also need to stay close, not let this become a simple execution from six feet away. I moved in a step. He took a step back and began circling, fists up like an inexperienced fighter who relies on overall bulk and strength too much.

It seemed like a good time for conversation, so I asked: "How'd you find me, Sarge?"

"Got a lot of friends."

"Neighbors?"

"None of your fucking business," he said. "I figured you might try something stupid. I told you to butt out. Now we end this, see?"

I'd seen this movie before. Lasko's ego was trumping training and judgment. Given his occupation—the legal one—I was pretty sure he had a gun, even while he was out of his jurisdiction and off duty. Given his other apparent occupation, which I didn't understand yet, I was even more certain he'd have a gun. Maybe he didn't want to fire a shot if he didn't have to. Alert the neighbors. More than that, he probably just wanted to kick the shit out of me, kill me with his bare hands, and he figured he could. He was wrong about that. I hoped.

All this made me wonder what was in the van. I was starting to get an idea. It didn't make much sense. Then I considered the fact that I was in the middle of a fight to the death, decided I'd better concentrate.

Lasko came at me with a big right hook. I blocked it with

my left forearm and ducked to avoid his attempt to grab me with his left. He had a surprised look on his face, but quickly narrowed his eyes and came at me with a left hook of similar style and intensity. I wanted to compliment him on being ambidextrous but instead blocked the punch with my right forearm and, knowing his moves now and seeing his rib cage exposed, I delivered a front snap kick that sounded like it snapped a rib.

The sergeant growled and cursed. Animalistic. He dug deep, surprising me with a left jab that got me squarely in the jaw. My lip burst and my head rocked back, but to a bystander it would've looked worse than it was. It was a punch from a big, strong puncher with a broken rib or two, and I didn't lose my senses.

I tasted the blood, like copper. That's when he reached behind his back, and I knew what he was going for. Unfortunately for Lasko he was off balance, leaning forward, legs wide apart. I delivered an obvious right roundhouse kick so he'd try to block it instead of grabbing the gun, and while he was busy blocking that kick and I was still airborne, my left foot connected hard between his legs. It wasn't elegant, it wasn't something Master Choi had taught me, at least not that target specifically, and I would never have done it in a match, but in a real fight you take what's given, and there they were.

Lasko doubled over, dropped to his knees, and grabbed at his crown jewels with both hands.

Half of me wanted to end it right there, and I knew I could. The other half of me really didn't want to kill a sheriff's sergeant just now. Sparing my knuckles, I took advantage of his incapacitated state and delivered a swift side kick to the side of his head, hoping it was just shy of deadly force. It was Lasko's turn to go airborne. He collapsed like a rag doll, a really big rag doll, three feet away, facedown. Tucked into his belt, at the small of his back, was a revolver. I removed it, ejected the shells, and threw the gun down the ravine where he wouldn't find it. Checked his pulse to make sure I hadn't terminated him.

I went back to the Jeep, looked at myself in the mirror. Lip bleeding all over my face, right eye and cheek swelling. I started the Jeep, turned it around and eased down the steep part of the ridge. The rocky terrain brought thuds of pain to my ribs. Bruised but not broken, I guessed.

Lasko would wake before long, maybe already, but he wouldn't have a gun, and I assumed he'd parked the white crew-cab somewhere on the drive leading up from Mr. '56's place, snuck from that ridge to this one. I'd have at least 15 minutes on him.

All was quiet on Deadman's Drive, the only dust my own. Skeleton Man and his oversized neighbor were nowhere to be seen. Lookouts, not fighters.

I drove back to Coldwater Canyon Road then north to the I-17 interchange. I crossed over to a frontage road on the other side of the freeway and drove south through the main business district of Black Canyon City. I blinked a couple times and was at the Black Canyon General Store & Pie. I pulled into the parking lot, found a tissue in the glove box and wiped most of the blood off my face, got out of the Jeep and went in through the general store entrance. The pies were in back on racks, still warm and smelling sticky sweet and crusty with hints of cinnamon and other spices. You'd have to try one to understand.

The two women at checkout looked at me funny, but didn't seem too surprised. I wasn't the first person they'd seen who had been punched in the face. The diverse establishment had a bar, too, frequented by Harley riders from out of town and some of the rougher locals. I fit right in today.

Peach, cherry, blueberry, and several others vied for my attention. I got apple. Sam's favorite. The younger woman at checkout rang me up, tried not to look at me and didn't say anything except "$17.95, please."

The older woman, in her sixties and maybe one of the owners, was smiling. "How's your day going, young man?"

"I think it's just getting started," I said.

"I'll pray for the other guy," she said.

CHAPTER 19

"You look like hell," Beach said, leaning back in his favorite chair on the outdoor patio, squeezing the red ball in his left hand.

"I feel worse," I said, my elbows on the table, fingers cradling my temples. It hurt to talk, and the words sounded like I'd been to the dentist. I hadn't noticed the pain until after I'd bought the pie and got back on I-17. Lip stung with any movement, jaw was giving me a headache, cheek and eye throbbed constantly. Ribs were fine as long as I didn't move. I knew it would all be healed in a few days, so I began to put the pain in a mental box.

Lulu's Grind was nearly empty. Lulu didn't serve dinner. And she didn't serve beer. I could've really used a beer. That's part of the reason I'd asked Beach to meet me here and not over at Café Amir, which had two excellent ales on tap. I had a feeling the beer would have to wait, no matter how loudly it called. Meanwhile, I wanted to be in a public place but one where we could talk without being overheard. I knew it was a risk, but it'd be risky going to my house or my office until I figured out the next step. Better to be in public. Even better with a posse member who packed a gun

97

and wasn't afraid to use it.

Lulu came out. "You look like hell," she said.

"Thanks, Lulu. Been a rough day."

"Been a rough year," she said.

Lulu knew more about me than just about anyone, except for Beach and Sam. Lulu and Jess had been best friends, did everything together, shared whatever women share that men generally aren't aware of. Presumably including a lot about me, especially the bad things. I could always tell Lulu knew way more about me than she let on.

She wagged a finger side-to-side, frowned, and gave me the head nod I knew well. "I tell you go have sex, not go fighting. It's time. A year is long enough."

I took a deep breath to acknowledge her good advice, wondered if Jess might advise the same. If anyone knew about that, it'd be Lulu. I might as well have plunged a knife into my ribs. I winced, let the breath out slowly.

"Can't argue with you, Lulu."

"Then listen to me." She bobbed her head once more as punctuation. "Now, what can I get for you?"

We both ordered coffee, and Lulu gave me one last stern look before heading inside.

***

I told Beach about the ranch, the van, the muffled shouts in Spanish, Skeleton Man and Mr. '56, the black BMW that might be the same one he'd seen, how Lasko had jumped me from behind, and how I had disabled and disarmed him. The talking was really painful, so I went slowly.

"Why didn't he just shoot you 'stead a sneakin' up on you?"

"Maybe he didn't want to make noise, attract attention," I said.

"Or maybe he's not so bright."

I nodded.

"And maybe he likes to fight."

I nodded.

"So you karate chopped his ass."

"Kicked him in the nuts."

"Works too."

"Then I kicked him in the head. He should be up by now, but he'll have a helluva headache." I was getting used to the pain of talking. That's the thing about pain. You can't always avoid it. Sometimes you just have to get used to it.

Lulu brought our coffees. We leaned back causally, as if we'd been chatting about fishing or basketball. Once she'd left we resumed.

"Why didn't you just shoot *him*?"

I shook my head. No need to verbalize this. Beach would understand.

"This isn't done," he said.

I shook my head in agreement.

"Something about that house, that van, a Maricopa County sheriff sergeant in plain clothes beating you up for being there," Beach said. "You want to see where this goes. So you neutralized him temporarily. Just enough force."

I put my thumb and forefinger together, left a tiny gap.

"And maybe a little bit more," Beach said.

I nodded and smiled. Smiling hurt worse than talking, so I stopped.

"You figure whatever's going on, you've just nudged it along."

I nodded.

"You know what it is that's going on?"

I shrugged.

"Ideas?"

I nodded.

***

Sam arrived and exchanged greetings with Beach.

"You look like hell," she said.

"Three's a charm," I said.

Lulu returned. Sam stood and they executed a light embrace coupled with a perfect single-side air kiss. My eyebrows must've shot up. I knew they knew each other. Sam and I had been here several times together, and Lulu knew all her regulars. But I didn't realize they were that friendly. My advanced detecting sensibilities smelled a serious conspiracy. They both looked at me, shook their heads and rolled their eyes like besties. Sam ordered a coffee and Lulu practically skipped away.

"What happened?" Sam asked.

"I was wondering the same thing," I said.

"I mean to your face."

I told her the whole story. Beach, having heard it already, rocked back on his chair and bounced the red ball off the patio tile.

Sam listened patiently until I was done.

"You kicked him in the nuts?"

I nodded.

"First case you're breaking noses, second case you're kicking a sheriff sergeant in the balls," she said. "You're going to get a reputation as a tough guy, you're not careful."

I gave her the "Aren't I?" look. She snorted out a laugh.

That's when I pulled the pie out of the bag and handed it to her.

"You didn't!"

I nodded. It was becoming my preferred means of communication.

"You just earned my services for a couple more hours," she said. "And I think I might know what was in the van."

I nodded. It was a gesture with many meanings.

"You're awfully quiet, Quinn," she said.

"Hurts," I said, pointing to my face.

I don't know exactly why she smiled at that. But I liked it, as always.

"What'd you find?"

"I dug deep on this," she said. "I tied some things together from several sources that I don't think anyone else has put together before. Ted McCall comes off as staunchly anti-immigrant, right? You've seen him on TV, the awful things he says."

"A donkey's hindquarters," Beach said.

"Agreed," Sam said. "He's been chasing immigrants for years, decades. Has apprehended a few. Even shot a couple without killing them. Got off on a self-defense claim. A sheriff deputy I know in Cochise County said there was some circumstantial evidence in another case that McCall shot and killed a border-crosser, but he was never arrested for it. Again, it wasn't publicized. So U.S. Border Control and local law enforcement agencies have an uneasy relationship with him. While they admit he, and his group, and others like them sometimes aid the cause of patrolling the border, they see the situation as a powder keg, and they can't condone vigilante patrols."

"So McCall's actions may be as violent as his words," I said.

"Fair bet, yes," she said. "His ideology has become a pathology."

"So you're inside his head a little more now."

"A little more."

"And your diagnosis?"

"Psychopaths and sociopaths both have a serious disregard for others," she said.

"Check," I said.

"They lie. They cheat."

"Let's assume he does."

"They're not always violent, but they can be."

"Check."

"And they don't feel remorse. Guilt is not in their vocabulary."

"Sounds like our guy," I said.

"McCall may have traits of both, but my bet is mostly psychopath," Sam said. "He uses others like pawns, but he manages to maintain relationships. People trust him."

"What's any of that got to do with the van?" Beach asked.

"I'm getting to that," Sam said. "You remember a few years back, when that SUV crashed, killed ten undocumented immigrants?"

"There were more than ten stuffed into it," Beach said.

"Seventeen," Sam said.

"How the hell do you put seventeen people into an SUV?" Beach said.

"I don't know," Sam said. "And I don't know how seven survived."

I rolled my hand to encourage Sam to get to the point.

"A Fed I know says the SUV was registered to a guy known to be close to McCall, an organizational lieutenant of sorts. Guy said his SUV had been stolen. The driver was undocumented, and he was killed, so the inquiry didn't go anywhere, and the details were never in the press."

"He's smuggling immigrants," I said.

"That's what was in the van," Beach said.

"Sure, steal my thunder," Sam said.

"He's running a safe house," I said.

"Or an unsafe one," Sam said.

"All right under the Feds' noses," I said. "Nobody would figure him for it."

"If I'm right," Sam said.

"You usually are."

"Usually."

"Let's go find out."

.

CHAPTER 20

The sun was thinking seriously about setting when I called Paul E. Peters and arranged to meet him halfway between Pleasant and his office. Beach, Sam and I had agreed to meet back at Lulu's Grind later.

When I left Lulu's I went a block east, one north, one west, then south back to Lulu's and looped around the traffic circle before heading to my house. Didn't see a tail. Slowed way down at the last turn before my home on Resolution Way so anyone following would maybe show themselves. Nothing.

I opened the garage door with my remote and pulled the Jeep inside. Solo met me in the garage, having come from the house through the doggie door. I'd made sure whenever Solo was home, he had free run of the house and garage, discouraging anyone who might think it a good idea to enter. I gave him a quick pat and told him to get in the Jeep. Opened a cabinet in the garage and grabbed the black case. It was light, wouldn't be a problem to carry on our hike. Put it in the Jeep, and Solo and I headed out of town.

I spotted Pauly's minivan in the parking lot of the shopping center just off the 101, parked next to it and climbed in through the sliding side door, black case in hand.

"This an official CIA vehicle?"

"Official shuttle-the-freaking-kids around van," Pauly said.

"That explains the Cheetos," I said, pointing into the crevice of the rear seat.

"You look like hell," he said.

I laughed. It hurt. I stopped.

Pauly shook his head. "So anyway, you going to tell me what this is about?"

"Nope."

Pauly nodded. I opened the case. He went to work. I let him. It took him just a few minutes.

"Going to use a little duct tape here," he said. "The fit isn't perfect. But it should work."

"You're a regular MacGyver," I said.

"Yeah, I once disarmed a missile with a paper clip. Saved most of Asia."

"Someday you're gonna have to tell me what you really do," I said.

"Someday I will," he said.

"Not today?"

"Nope."

I shut up and let him finish. He handed it to me like a proud father giving his son a toy he'd put together. Then he opened the center console and took out three pairs of night vision goggles, handed them to me.

"You did not get these from me," he said.

"Of course not. I picked them up at Radio Shack."

"Government issue, Quinn. You get caught with those, they'll waterboard you. Don't screw around."

I nodded.

"Mikey got anything to do with it?

I didn't answer.

"McCall?"

I didn't answer.

"You going to break any laws tonight?"

I shrugged.

"Then I don't want to know any more, do I?"

I shook my head.

"You need help?"

"Probably," I said.

"You going to ask me for any? I can bring the full force of the Feds to bear, if needed."

I wasn't sure if Pauly was serious or not. I looked him in the eyes. No hint of joking.

"I got backup," I said. "I'll be fine. Keep your cell phone handy though, in case I need a MacGyverism on the fly."

Pauly nodded, sharp and serious-like, and I guessed that his "full force of the Feds" was not an empty promise.

"You'll need to allow for the extra weight," he said. "It's just a couple ounces, but it'll make a difference. And remember, at full resolution with a live feed you'll have less battery life. Whatever you're doing, make it quick."

CHAPTER 21

"Smuggling immigrants from Mexico and Central America into the United States is complicated," Sam explained. "It's big business, well organized, run more and more by Mexican drug cartels."

I knew most of this, but Sam was a reporter, and she'd been researching all this for me. I was her audience, so I listened intently. Beach and Solo were in the back of the Jeep as we drove across the 101 and then up I-17. With the top down, they couldn't hear Sam. But we'd all discussed the plan already, so that was OK. This was just background.

"There are networks of people in Mexico whose sole job is to round up potential migrants, with promises that may or may not be legitimate," she explained. "The migrants are brought to the border in busloads, sometimes put up in motels. They wait on someone else in the organization, known as a coyote, to take them across. The coyote's only goal is to make it to a border town on this side, dump the cargo and collect his fees before getting caught."

"Then what?" A good listener knows when to insert a useful prompt.

"The immigrants are moved around, maybe put up in

different motels for a while, maybe transported to a safe house. That's typically owned by someone known as the boss. The boss is the smuggling organization's top dog."

Night was coming on fast, just a hint of purple left to silhouette the mountains to the west. I was anxious to get there.

"Used to be the smugglers, especially the coyotes, relied on their reputations of success and good treatment of the migrants. Word of mouth got them their next clients. So they had incentive to treat the migrants well. With the drug cartels getting involved, the smuggling is mixing with drugs and the sex trade. The migrants are promised safe passage and a good job in the promised land, but as often as not they get nothing of the sort."

"They make them work for years to pay off the exorbitant smuggling fee," I said.

"Or worse, they'll turn the women and children into sex slaves or prostitutes."

This I didn't know so much about. My jaw clenched tight and I gripped the wheel tighter. I tried but failed to relax. We had a good plan in place, even if we didn't know exactly what we'd find.

"What's in it for someone like McCall?"

"A crossing can cost two grand or more," Sam said. "He might get a cut of that."

"Or he's selling sex slaves."

"You sure you want to wade into the middle of this?"

I pushed the pedal down and took the Jeep up to eighty.

***

It was pitch black when we exited at Coldwater Canyon Road in Black Canyon City. Just as the road doubled back to the south I turned left and wound through a maze of small streets to reconnect with another segment of Coldwater Canyon that headed east. I was pretty sure it would be a bad move to take Deadman's Drive out to McCall's place. Skeleton Man and Mr. '56 would be on the lookout, and who knows who else. So we'd mapped an approach that would bring us within a mile of the ranch on the north side, via a road of unknown condition. From there we would walk. Google Maps showed there were no houses the last half-mile of the road, so if we played it right, we could approach unnoticed.

We followed Coldwater Canyon Road nearly to its end, found the rutted unmarked road forking off to the southeast. I cut the lights and drove slowly. The road gave way to rough terrain, the bumps jarring. I drove until I worried we'd get stuck. I turned the Jeep around so it'd be ready for a quick getaway if needed.

We got out. Solo hopped to the ground and was immediately at my heel. I grabbed the black case that sat in the back between Beach and Solo.

"That way," I whispered and pointed. It was slow walking in the dark, the milky sea of stars not helping much.

We walked in silence toward a slight rise in the otherwise flat valley. If I had it figured right, McCall's place would be just a couple hundred yards beyond the rise, and we wouldn't be visible from this side of it. It was so dark, we wouldn't be seen anyway, unless someone was looking for us and shone a powerful light our way. Off to the right, far in the distance, I saw a porch light that should be Skeleton Man's place. Beyond that a few other lights dotted the night.

We walked bent over for the last twenty yards, then stayed crouched down and peeked over the rise. Nothing.

Beach asked in a whisper: "Bearings wrong?"

"Nope," I said.

"Where is it?" Sam asked.

"Right there." I pointed.

"Where?" they both whispered together.

"Look harder," I said.

You actually had to look slightly away from the house to

see its dark geometry against the unlit desert. No lights on.

Beach asked the obvious question: "They gone?"

"Let's find out," I said.

I opened the black case and pulled out the drone I'd built two years ago. Pauly had replaced the regular video camera with an infrared one, which would pick up heat rather than regular light. I hadn't flown it in two years, so I'd be rusty. I'd inserted a new battery that was fully charged, but Pauly had warned me it wouldn't last long with the extra weight and the camera.

A few minutes was all we needed.

I set the drone on a flat spot of ground and turned it on, paired my iPhone with the drone's onboard Wi-Fi. From my phone I could see what the drone saw—nothing but a dark grey screen, since the camera pointed at a forty-five-degree angle toward the ground.

The iPhone signaled the drone's four rotors to spin, and with a quiet whir the machine lifted off, automatically hovering three feet above the ground to await further instruction. The app showed me what direction the drone was facing, its altitude above the ground, and its distance from us. Flying it on a pitch black night would not be easy.

I took it up to twenty feet and moved it a ways to the southeast, toward the McCall ranch house. Hovered it again, then rotated it slowly 360 degrees. The screen was black, black, black, then suddenly lit up bright white with what appeared to be three people and a dog, then black, black, black until it was back in its original position, facing southeast.

Despite the silent night, the drone was not particularly noisy from this distance. I took it up to a hundred feet and a little farther out, and we could barely hear it. I flew it slowly, blindly, toward the target. Within seconds we couldn't hear it at all.

After a couple minutes the screen lit up briefly, a blip on the left side that was quickly gone. I commanded the drone to hover. It took me a moment to get it to fly backward. The blip came and went again. The drone inched forward slightly, hovered, swiveled to the left. The blip came into focus, far away, but clearly a horse. I tilted the drone up slightly. Two other horses came into view. A slight turn to the right revealed partial outlines of the ranch house, dull but noticeable, especially on the western side, where the afternoon sun's heat must have been stored in the block walls.

Sam and Beach looked over my shoulders. Solo didn't seem overly interested in the infrared image, but he sat patient and alert. I was pretty sure he knew something was up. Heck, we'd discussed the plan in front of him.

About ten feet outside the front door someone stood sentry, didn't move. I couldn't make out much detail, only enough to be sure it was a human. Someone else was outside the back entrance, walking in random patterns within a small area.

"Guarding the front and rear," Beach whispered. "Guy in front's a pro. Guy in back's bored. What's that?" He pointed to a faintly glowing rectangle in the back of the house, northeast corner.

"Maybe they've got a fireplace going in that room," I said.

"It's still eighty-five degrees out," Sam pointed out.

"What else would create that much warmth?" Beach said, but we all knew the likely answer.

I pointed to two vehicles out front. The fact that we could see one clearly in infrared meant it had arrived recently, engine still warm.

"Looks like a pickup," I said.

"And the other one?"

"Hard to tell. It's barely warmer than the background. I'm guessing BMW."

"Can you get a closer look?" Beach asked.

I flew the drone straight ahead to what I figured was a

good two hundred feet from the back door. We could see the man outside more clearly now. Definitely a man, average height but thick in the chest, an apparent pile of muscle. He stopped pacing and looked up, put his hand on his hip, maybe a gun there. I backed the drone off. He looked left, right, seemed to be listening, then ran his left hand through his hair, removed his hand from his hip, and resumed pacing. *Tough Guy No. 1.*

"Around front?"

I maneuvered the drone in a circle around the west side to the front, careful to hold the ranch house in view and keep the drone beyond hearing range. The bigger man in front came into clearer focus. Bigger than the guy in the back. Arms folded. Back ramrod straight. If he hadn't lit up in infrared, I'd have thought him a statue. I couldn't tell if he was wearing sunglasses, but I knew who it was. Didn't see a gun, but knew there was one, and where it was.

A pair of headlights appeared on Deadman's Drive. We didn't need the drone's infrared to see them. The vehicle turned toward the ranch house. The height and position of the headlights gave it away.

"Same van I saw earlier today," I said. "Eighty percent odds anyway."

"Call for backup?" Sam said.

"No time," I said. "They know I know something. They don't know what, but they're not stupid. They waited for darkness and they're going to clear out. Based on the size of the van, there could be thirty or forty people in that room, and if we don't do something, well, you know."

Beach and Sam nodded. I hit a button and we discussed the situation while the drone flew itself back to us.

"So there's at least three of them," Beach said.

"Probably four," I said. "Could be more."

"These operations usually involve small groups," Sam said. "The fewer that know what's going on, the better."

"Let's assume four," I said.

"And there are four of us," Beach said, a well-deserved compliment to Solo, who wagged his tail in appreciation.

"We'll have to make it work," Sam said.

"They have a plan, they know what they're gonna do next," Beach said.

"But they don't know what we're gonna do," I pointed out.

"What are we gonna do?"

"Can you handle Lasko?"

"I'll talk sense into him," Beach said. "He won't be expecting that. I'm in uniform, and it'll confuse him. Might at least occur to him that the whole cavalry is with me."

"But it isn't."

"But he doesn't know that. I just need him to hesitate."

"And if he draws on you?"

"I'll be expecting it."

"His gun is in the small of his back, Butch. Watch for it."

"Thanks Sundance."

"A shootout at the McCall Corral," I said.

"You bet your britches."

"Can we get back to work here?" Sam said.

I sighed. "Be careful, old friend."

I turned to Sam. "You and Solo got the guy in back. You don't need to get close enough for him to see or hear you. Just turn Solo loose. You know the command?"

"I got it," Sam said.

We discussed the timing, how it all might go down relatively peacefully under Plan A or, if needed, the dramatically less peaceful Plan B. We quietly went over the bird signals Beach would make. They'd be fishy sounding, but we just needed a few seconds to enact the entire plan.

"They'll all have guns," Beach said, pulling his out of its holster, clicking the safety off.

"You have a gun," I said.

"You two don't," he said.

He reached into his boot and took out another pistol,

tried to hand it to Sam. She declined. "I've got Solo," she said. "And I don't know how to use one of those anyway."

He tried to give the gun to me. I shook my head firmly. He shook his, resignedly.

"Goddamn karate cowboy," he said.

"Taekwondo," I whispered. "Let's go."

I boxed the drone up quickly and we left it there. I didn't know when, or if, I'd be retrieving it.

.

CHAPTER 22

Were put on our night vision goggles, walked as low as we could and still be quiet but swift. About fifty yards from the ranch house, we split up, Scooby Doo style. Beach went right, to circle around front. I went left, to circle in behind and to the east of Tough Guy No. 1, as close to the back door as I could get without him noticing me. Solo stayed with Sam.

We couldn't know what to expect inside, but we'd agreed on a likely scenario. There was a room full of immigrants, behind a locked door that might be locked, about to be moved to the van. If they were in fact locked away, they'd be a non-factor. If they were already on the move, the whole thing could turn into a nightmare.

Lasko was out front, standing guard. Tough Guy No. 1 was doing the same out back. Ted McCall was presumably inside, or driving the van. Three minimum, likely four. There was only one vehicle out front besides the white van, so we weren't expecting an army.

Their tactical decision to turn the lights off, make it look like nobody was home, was to our advantage. We had night-vision. We knew where two of them were. They were on guard, but they didn't know we were here or what we had planned.

With my goggles I could see a faint outline of the house. Tough Guy No. 1 was visible as day. I approached silently. The horses whinnied and I froze. Tough Guy stopped pacing, looked into the dark night. I knew he wouldn't see anything, but I could tell he was agitated. He ran his left hand through his hair. Twice. Pulled the gun off his right hip and struck the classic pose of a cornered criminal, crouched and frightened. Not as tough as he'd seemed in my office. Maybe not used to using a gun so much.

I found a rain barrel close to the house, crept up and crouched behind it. Everything was silent.

Less than a minute passed before I heard Beach's bird whistle, faint but obvious. It was a pretty bad imitation of an unknown bird, but Bad Guy No. 1 either didn't hear it or didn't think anything of it. I listened a tense moment for the second whistle indicating Lasko was under arrest, the signal for Sam to release Solo. Knowing Lasko, I wasn't really expecting a whistle. And sure enough, there was a gunshot instead. Then another. I hoped they were from the right gun.

Bad Guy No. 1 froze. Solo made almost no sound as he covered the fifty yards, quick as a bunny, and blindsided him. Solo barked once and had his teeth in the guy's face and a good growl going while I sprinted to the back door. I was ready to risk my right shoulder to bust it down, but the doorknob worked just as well.

I came in low and hollered "McCall!" just as a deafening shotgun blast lit the room and peppered the door jamb above my head. I dove ahead and to my left behind a couch. Two more shots rang out, the pellets wasted on the wall behind me.

Three shots. If the shotgun was legal, he'd have to reload. Iffy, but I had to think and act quickly. There'd been no other shots fired, no shouts between men. I used my powers of deduction to conclude that McCall was by himself and I had only seconds to do something or become a target again. I turned my phone on and raised it above the couch. My phone didn't get shot. I brought the phone down, moved to the left and raised my head up enough to see the heat signature of a good-sized man fumbling to reload a shotgun in the dark. Another man, smaller, crouched against the wall just inside the front door. I bounded over the couch, took two steps and launched into an awkward, flying kick that would have embarrassed Master Choi. Just as the larger man was swinging the gun back at me, my feet struck his chest. He flew backward and lost the gun. I fell inelegantly to the hard floor, added a bruised hip to the injury list.

The kick had been pathetic, and he was on his feet quickly. He flicked a wall switch and a light came on, blinding me. I tore the goggles off, blinked and was pounded to the floor by his shoulder. My whole upper body suffered the impact. My ribs complained loudest.

It was definitely Ted McCall. He was tough, had fighting skills, and wasn't afraid to use them. I knew it beforehand because I'd looked it up. I knew it now because he was kicking my ass. I also knew I did not want to wrestle. But here he was, straddling me and pinning my right shoulder to the floor and about to finish the job. I didn't have many moves left.

Fortunately, McCall's moves were of the classic Western variety. He wound up his right arm to deliver the knockout punch, and before he connected I shoved the palm of my left hand at lightning speed into his lower jaw. Broken, I was pretty sure. His jaw, I mean. My hand was fine. I used the soft, meaty part. As his head rocked to the side, his punch still landed, modestly, on the side of my face, popping my lip back open and seriously adding to the pain of my already sore cheekbone. Maybe broken, I wasn't sure.

I growled out a battle cry and somehow kept my focus in

the face of intense pain.

He was straddling me and swung again. I caught his forearm and used the momentum of the punch, with a little help from my legs, to throw him off me. His punch hit the floor. Knuckles broke loudly as he flew from my grip. I was on my feet but he was already scrambling at me. When he lunged for my legs I delivered a simple but rock-hard front snap kick that snapped his head back and knocked him out. I knew instantly it was done.

Only when he went limp did I realize that I'd delivered a kick meant to kill, not subdue. Part of me worried I might actually have killed him. Most of me didn't care.

Beach was standing by the front door, watching, his gun pointed at the unarmed, evidently terrified Michael Derbin Smith, who was still crouched by the wall.

"Don't worry," I said to Beach, putting my hands on my knees to catch my breath. "I got this."

"I coulda shot your guy," Beach said, pointing his pistol at McCall, "but it looked like you had it under control."

"Totally," I said.

He used his boot to get Mikey face down on the floor, zipped his hands together behind his back with a plastic tie, then hustled out the back door.

"That's a helluva dog," I heard him say.

"Down, Solo," Sam said.

The growling stopped.

Sam walked in. Solo burst past her and headed straight for Ted McCall and began barking. It was the first time I'd ever heard him bark more than once. He wouldn't stop.

"Down, Solo."

He barked again, looked at me like I was an idiot. Barked once more.

"I know, buddy, I know. Down."

Solo backed off, looked like he was about to argue with me, then, finally, sat. Whined a bit.

"There's our drone pilot," I said to Sam.

I fished through McCall's pockets. He was still breathing. I had mixed emotions about that. I found keys, tossed them to Sam and pointed to the door in the northwest corner of the room.

"Everything is OK," Sam said in Spanish. She tried three keys until she found one that worked, opened the door and turned on the light. "Don't worry. We're here to help you."

I couldn't see inside the room, and Sam just stood there a moment, didn't say anything. Then, finally: "About sixty," she said over her shoulder. "All women and children."

I stood over Ted McCall. Every muscle in my body tensed.

"Don't," Sam said. She was at my side. The migrants were filing out, dirty, looking scared and hungry.

I took a deep breath and looked at Sam. She'd been calm throughout. Now she was trembling.

"Everything's OK now," I said. "You just said so yourself."

"Except now you *really* look like hell," she said.

Beach came back in, cuffed McCall, got on his cell and made the requisite call for backup that we no longer needed.

I look at Sam, then looked down. Next to her was a girl, maybe six, with long, dark, tangled hair that looked like it hadn't been brushed or washed in weeks. She had adult-sized brown eyes on a small round face with strong cheekbones. I motioned to Sam with my eyes. Sam looked down. The girl looked up. Sam put her arm around the girl, and the girl leaned in. Solo came over, licked the girl's hand, then sat.

I didn't know what to do next.

Sam did.

She moved in, put her other arm around me, her head on my chest, and squeezed.

"Ouch," I said.

She was still trembling. She squeezed a little tighter. It hurt like hell and felt damn good. I didn't say ouch again.

CHAPTER 23

After a late-night visit to the emergency room, some stitches and X-rays, I learned I was the lucky one. One broken rib, otherwise just bad bruises. Ted McCall was in intensive care, expected to pull through. I had roughly zero emotion in response to that news. I was more interested in Jackie Brand's condition.

"She came out of the coma this morning," Sam said. "They think she'll be OK."

I nodded. Sam didn't see it. We were sitting next to each other, our feet on the flagstone rim of the fireplace, both watching Pinnacle Peak, splashed with the orange of a setting sun. Solo was curled up on the other side of the fire pit, one eye flicking back and forth as each of us spoke. I had a strong painkiller in my system that wasn't working too well, except to make me tired and a little off-balance, and two shots of straight gin were kicking in. I could feel the pulse of a throb in my jaw and cheek, but it was subsiding into a sensation other than pain.

"Why'd he try to kill her?" I asked. "I still don't get that part."

I had it mostly outlined, but by now Sam would have it

all worked out.

"Allegedly," Sam corrected me.

"Why'd he allegedly try to kill her?"

"You're the detective," Sam said.

"You're the reporter." She had interviewed some of the immigrants, been working on the story all day, and it was online now. I was too woozy to read it.

"The immigration system has more side effects than most people realize," she explained.

"A lot of immigrant women are on their own. An undocumented woman has a harder time getting help from the immigration system. It's harder for her to get a work visa, she's less likely to be given political asylum. If an immigrant woman's husband is arrested, she's suddenly even more vulnerable, maybe has no way of supporting herself. If she's abused, by her husband or by someone she's been enslaved too, she's got no way to prove it. The person abusing her may be undocumented, so she can't even prove he exists or that she lives with him. She and her children end up taking whatever help comes their way."

"Opportunity," I said.

"Exactly, the root of most crime. Sheriff Otto's roundups tend to catch more men than women and children. Apparently some bad cops have arrangements to find the wife and kids who're left behind. Others are engaged at simply diverting women and children as they cross the border.

"To McCall."

"Or people like him, who'll then sell them or rent them out to pimps around the valley."

"Change how illegal immigration is dealt with…."

"…McCall loses his supply."

"Jackie Brand wanted to end the roundups."

"Bad for business," Sam said.

"McCall had a great cover. Last guy you'd suspect of human trafficking."

"Maybe not the last."

"But not the first."

"No way," she said.

"Enough evidence to convict?"

"The footprint photos will help," she said. "They'll probably make a deal with Mikey for his testimony."

"Lasko?"

"Looks like he was one of those bad cops, but as it stands the evidence is circumstantial."

"Him being dead makes it hard to go to trial."

"Indeed. And maybe saves Otto's ass."

"Otto involved?"

"We'll never know," she said.

"Slippery bastard."

"Indeed," she said. "But honestly, I don't figure him for it."

"Much as he'd like to see Jackie Brand out of the picture, he's probably smart enough not to order a hit on a politician."

"Probably," she said.

"Beach doing all right?"

"He figures he'll get a formal reprimand for doing law stuff in another county, and there will be the routine internal investigation triggered when any officer fires his weapon. There probably won't be a parade, but he's not expecting to get fired or jailed. He said to tell you to expect a full inquiry on what the hell you think you were doing, but he put a good word in for you and said to call him if you need bail money."

"He did good," I said, swallowing some sudden emotions related to the danger I'd put the two of them in. "You too."

"And Solo," she said. His ears perked up.

"And Solo." His ears perked up again.

"Quinn?"

I listened. We stared at Pinnacle Peak. She didn't finish

the thought.

"I know," I said. "But it worked out. I'm OK. You're OK. We're here. We did something worth doing."

"Let's not do it like that again. I don't know if I can."

"Sure you can," I said. "But we'll try not to."

Without looking, I reached out with my left hand and found her right. Her palm was up, resting on the arm of the chair. Her fingers were curled up slightly. I brushed her fingers, then let my fingers rest in her palm. She let me. I wasn't sure how she'd react. I wasn't sure how I'd react. A moment went by, everything and nothing. Then it occurred to me that I hadn't thought of Jess in that moment, nor at all in the past 24 hours. As I let the memories and images come in, they didn't shake me like they used to. They were warm and pleasant. I was comfortable with them being there, and Jess seemed OK with it, too, so I let them linger, then fade.

Sam was still. The quiet got quieter. I felt a small but distinct electric current run from her palm, through my fingers to my shoulders and down my spine. Then she curled her fingers and squeezed mine. And I let her.

ABOUT THE AUTHOR

Robert Roy Britt is the author of *Closure* and *Drone*, the first two books in the Eli Quinn detective series, and the short prequel *Murder Mountain*. He lives in Arizona with his wife, their youngest son and two dogs. You can visit his website at robertroybritt.com.

If you liked this book, please review it on Amazon, Goodreads or wherever you get bookish. Reviews help sell books and allow Eli Quinn to take on more cases.

ACKNOWLEDGEMENTS

I'm indebted to my sharp-eyed editor, Lauren Craft, for fixes big and small. To my fellow authors at the Internet Writing Workshop—Mark, Robin, Silvia, Jennifer, Elaine, Bob, Mairhi, Carmel, Michele, Bill, Virginia, Francene, Elma, Tim and others—a huge thanks for your enthusiasm, expertise and encouragement. Your critiques helped shape and sharpen this story in too many ways to count. And Mom, you're an awesome beta reader. Solo digs you.